"FOR LAUGHS, STICK WITH MS. PIESMAN, who is hilariously articulate on the anxieties of smart single women on the make in an indifferent universe."
—*The New York Times Book Review*

"[A] WILDLY FUNNY WHODUNIT . . . Share the laughter; have a friend around so you can read aloud the good bits that occur about every second sentence."
—*The Drood Review*

HIGH PRAISE FOR
MARISSA PIESMAN'S
SURVIVAL INSTINCTS
AND THE ACCLAIMED NINA FISCHMAN
MYSTERY SERIES

"WRY, INSIGHTFUL . . . Marissa Piesman's New York is a wonderland of wisecracks, great Chinese delivery, and hip Jewish mothers who stay up late to critique Letterman."   —*New York Newsday*

"A TERRIFIC MURDER STORY, with so many false leads skillfully planted, the audience will not be able to stop turning the pages until the villain is finally revealed!"
—*Internet Bookwatch*

"Baby boomers and parents will instantly appreciate Nina and Ida's banter . . . Piesman may write mysteries, but her humor and social insights suggest Nora Ephron, Fran Lebowitz, and even a touch of Jane Austen." —*Booklist*

"FOR SHEER FUN, MARISSA PIESMAN'S NINA FISCHMAN MYSTERIES ARE AMONG THE MOST CONSISTENTLY ENTERTAINING IN THE FIELD."
—*The Plain Dealer* (Cleveland)

Alternate Sides
Close Quarters
Heading Uptown
Personal Effects
Unorthodox Practices
The Yuppie Handbook
(with Marilee Hartley)

SURVIVAL INSTINCTS

MARISSA PIESMAN

A DELL BOOK

Published by
Dell Publishing
a division of
Bantam Doubleday Dell Publishing Group, Inc.
1540 Broadway
New York, New York 10036

The trademark Dell® is registered in the U.S. Patent
and Trademark Office.

ISBN 0-440-22453-5

Reprinted by arrangement with Delacorte Press

Printed in the United States of America

Published simultaneously in Canada

November 1997

10 9 8 7 6 5 4 3 2 1

WCD

AUTHOR'S NOTE

I wish to thank my brother, Dr. Joseph Piesman, Chief of the Lyme Disease Vector Section of the Centers for Disease Control and Prevention in Fort Collins, Colorado. He offered invaluable assistance and guidance while I attempted to create descriptions of a world of which I know nothing. Thanks also go to my agent, Janet Manus, my editor, Jackie Farber, and the home team, Jeff and Leah Marks, for cooperation, love, and support all around.

CHAPTER ONE

NINA WAS SITTING right behind the wing of a 737 that had attained its cruising altitude of 35,000 feet. So far there had been little turbulence, lunch had been edible (Nina had low standards), and the middle seat remained unoccupied, all making for a pleasant flight. But best of all was the fact that the plane was pointed directly away from LAX.

She'd lose three hours today because of the time difference. But then, she'd just lost three months of her life sitting around Los Angeles, waiting for Jonathan to come home every evening. Trying to drive, trying to adjust. Nina had finally slipped up too close against a serious depression and it had scared her. So one Tuesday evening, when she realized that she had become too immobilized to floss her teeth, she caught Jonathan before he was even through the door.

"I've really got to leave now," she said.

"Where are you going?" He threw his briefcase onto the dining room table, as was his nightly custom.

"Home. Back to New York."

"Oh. How come? Is something wrong?"

"Everything's wrong."

"Well, I'm sorry to hear that."

She'd expected him to react defensively. But he *was* somewhat at fault, working all the time and barely listening to her, no matter what she was talking about. Jonathan was nervous about his job. Sure, that was understandable. And he *had* been very generous to Nina, not pressuring her to work or cook or clean or function in any way. And she hadn't.

She just couldn't function in California. She could barely breathe. Nina tried to explain this to him, on that hot Tuesday evening during a month that was allegedly October, but it all came out in a messy gush. She had just come around to "It's not really your fault" for the third time when she caught his eyes flickering anxiously over to his briefcase.

In all fairness, his eyes flickered right back to reestablish contact, but it was too late. That fraction of a second was enough to remind her that she'd never be more than a chapter in Jonathan Harris's book. It was her own self she'd have to read to the end. Which was why Nina now found herself aloft, approaching the Pittsburgh airport, losing three hours but gaining her old life back. Minus job and apartment, of course, both of which she'd trashed in the scurry to follow Jonathan out West.

It was the apartment that had gone first. Well, if she had to be completely honest about it, the trash was where that dump belonged. Windows that didn't close, faucets that didn't turn, an intercom that couldn't com. So she moved across the park into Jonathan's glossy high-rise and tried to learn to be an East Sider. She had barely gotten around to comparing the indigenous varieties of bagels, however, when Jonathan's ad agency transferred him to California. The transfer had been on and off for a year, and by that time their households had been fully merged.

She could have sublet, she supposed, instead of terminating her lease. But it had seemed pathetic to sublet such a drafty, drippy place. The general rule was not to burn your bridges behind you. But shouldn't a bridge with a glaring structural defect be set ablaze?

And she supposed she could have applied for a leave of absence from her job when she decided to move out West. But her work had its drafty, drippy aspects as well. So she threw it into the bonfire along with her therapy group, her gym membership, and most of her old shoes.

Coming back to New York was going to be a little tricky without a job or an apartment. Manhattan wasn't the kind of place where people had spare rooms. There was only one person of Nina's acquaintance who actually had an extra bedroom and that was her mother.

Ida Fischman might not have lived a privileged existence for most of her decades, but she had gotten lucky in real estate late in life, cashing in on the co-op fever that raged through Manhattan's housing stock in the 1980s. So there she was, snugly ensconced in a two bedroom co-op on West End Avenue, with clean sheets in the guest room and a coffeemaker that made an eight-cup pot.

Moving back in with your parents had become common among recent college graduates. So much so that the media was referring to them as the boomerang generation. But Nina was too old to qualify as a boomerang. She was a solid baby boomer, born during the Eisenhower administration, a veteran of dorm rooms and roommates and tiny studio apartments. Sure, she occasionally had to spend a night at Ida's house, when her boiler broke or when she had her wisdom teeth extracted. But never had she actually placed an item of clothing in one of the empty drawers in the guest room. Now she would have no choice.

Wednesday morning she had called a few airlines to find a cheap transcontinental flight that would get her out of there quickly. Everyone was pretty booked up except for USAir. The reservations clerk was friendly and courteous and Nina found herself treating the woman as her personal savior. "Yes, thank you, thank you," Nina kept repeating. "Tomorrow would be fine. Perfect in fact."

The next call was harder to make. Ida picked up on the second ring.

"Surprise, surprise," Nina said.

"Where are you?" Ida said, as if she knew something.

"I'm still in L.A. But I'm coming home tomorrow."

"For good?" her mother asked, as if she *really* knew something.

"Actually, yes. For good. I'm flying into LaGuardia. I get in around ten."

"LaGuardia?"

"Yeah, the only flight I could get on short notice was on USAir. Famous for their crashes."

"Good luck. You'll have to change planes in Pittsburgh."

"Of course." Nina knew that her mother wasn't really thinking about USAir or Pittsburgh or LaGuardia. Ida was merely biding her time until Nina came to her with the real explanation. They both knew that now was not the time. "So . . . um . . . Ma?"

"Yeah?"

"Would it be all right if I stay in your apartment for a while?"

"Of course. Can you manage all your luggage?"

"Yeah, I'll take a cab."

Nina had put most of her stuff in storage before she headed for California—her books, her couch, and thirteen boxes of tchotchkes wrapped in old newspapers. But there were a couple of suitcases down in the belly of the plane that contained items that Nina had to remain in close proximity to. Like her pantyhose collection. She couldn't let that out of her sight.

Other women could dash into the drugstore and snatch a one-size-fits-all in a color they liked. Not Nina. One size fit all except if you were shaped like a Fischman. Nina had spent years tracking down good-looking pantyhose that didn't bag around the ankles but still made the trip up over her hips and thighs.

Actually, she couldn't complain. Queen-size pantyhose had come a long way in the past few years. Up from the depths of that horrible orangey nude beige, soaring to the heights of mulberry and stone and brushed silver. There was no definite seminal event that the fat liberation movement could claim, like Stonewall, for anniversary celebrations and such. But the day someone decided to put out a line of queen-size stockings in decent colors probably came as close as anything else.

So here was Nina, forty years old, with her pantyhose collection packed away in her nonmatching luggage, changing planes to fly home to move in with her widowed, pensioned mother and be unemployed.

As Nina sat with a cup of coffee in the antiseptic expanses of the Pittsburgh USAir terminal, waiting for her flight to LaGuardia to board, she tried to make some plans for the future. What kind of job to look for, who to call, how to network. But this tiny residual sob was lodged in her chest and it kept turning her mind back to how miserable she had been in Los Angeles. She hadn't cried so much since her first summer at Camp Wel-Met. She'd lie down on Jonathan's couch in the afternoon, staring up at the ceiling and the tears would stream down into her ears. She'd have to shake her head to get the water out, as if she'd just done a few laps in the pool.

It had scared her. She felt better already, even though she was alone in Pittsburgh, with that residual little sob still there. But at least she was confident of its residuality. She knew that the tiny sob was not going to mushroom into a huge choking thing, that her eyes would not turn red, her throat would not become raw, and her ears had filled with tears for the last time. Even though she had done a slash-and-burn number on her old life, leaving her a woman without a zip code, a woman with a yearly income that consisted of the interest on a five-thousand-dollar certificate of deposit, she knew she would survive. Because she was doing what she had to do. Nina was coming home.

CHAPTER
TWO

IT WAS PAST MIDNIGHT by the time Nina got to her mother's house, so she told the doorman not to ring upstairs. She had the key to let herself in. But Ida was still awake, eating her late-night snack of Special K and watching *David Letterman*. Nina dumped her bags right inside the door.

"Is that you?" Ida called from the eat-in kitchen, where a countertop eight-inch Sony was piping out the aging-hipster sounds of Paul Shaffer's band. Nina had never thought that she'd have to move in with her mother at age forty. But if you had to do something like that, she told herself, at least it helped to have a mother who watched *Letterman*.

"Yeah, it's me." Nina headed down the hall and stopped at the kitchen threshold. "Who's on *Letterman*?"

"Kathie Lee Gifford. But I think you missed her."

"Aw, shucks. She's my favorite. The Nancy Reagan of the nineties."

"She's not so bad. Letterman brings out the best in her. Anyway, how are you?" Ida gave her a hug and a kiss.

"Terrible."

"Well, you look terrible."

"Thank you. I've spent three months crying into my ears."

"Crying into your beer? You mean you've taken to drink?"

"No, but it might have been a good idea. I wish I'd thought of it. It would have been more fun." Nina liked to drink, but didn't have the stuff of a true alcoholic, since it rarely occurred to her to hit the bottle. She could never remember about the existence of alcohol. When times were tough, she was more likely to hit the telephone. Now that she was back in New York, she could whine and kvetch at local rates. The thought gave her courage. "Actually," Nina said, "I think I'll have a drink. What have you got?"

"Whatever you want." Ida opened a kitchen cabinet. "Grand Marnier, Cherry Marnier, Drambuie, crème de cassis, and some vodka. Plain and cranberry."

"Jesus." Her mother's liquor inventory was more likely to give you cavities than cirrhosis. "What are you supposed to do with cranberry vodka?"

"I don't know. I bought it because it looked so pretty."

"Forget it. I'll just have some Robitussin."

"Don't be silly. Have some Drambuie on ice. It's delicious."

"Goes well with Special K, huh?"

"As a matter of fact," Ida said, "it does." She picked up a plastic tumbler and poured an inch of Drambuie. Nina never understood why her mother persisted in using non-breakable glasses, as if it were 1958 and there were still toddlers in the house. Perhaps it was Ida's way of staying young, a method of her own device, instead of dyeing her hair or lifting her face. Ida never looked old to Nina. Her hair had been gray for decades and her body had had the same plump pear shape for as long as her daughter could remember. The eyeglasses had always been thick and the shoes had always been comfortable. It was as if Ida Fischman had decided to get her aging over with before menopause so that she wouldn't have to deal with both things at once.

Ida took the cup of Drambuie over to the refrigerator and opened the freezer. She kept a large supply of ice cubes in several neatly stacked Ziploc plastic bags. She reached for one and unzipped it.

"Ma, why do you keep so much ice in there?" Nina asked. "You know you never use it. The ice cubes you're holding now were probably frozen sometime during Ronald Reagan's first term in office."

"It's good to have some ice on hand. You never know."

"What for—in case the cossacks come to get you, they should have a cold drink?"

"What else am I going to do with all the space in my freezer? It's not like I'm keeping chuck roasts in there." She handed Nina her Drambuie.

Nina took a sip. It was silly to pretend that the stuff was too sweet for her. It was delicious. She downed some more. "Now, let me get this straight. You don't want your freezer space going to waste, is that it?"

"Waste not, want not."

"But freezer space? Would you go out and buy more clothing just because your closets weren't full enough?"

Ida shrugged. "It's not an issue."

"That's for sure." Ida still had the dress that Nina had worn to her cousin Richie's bar mitzvah in 1964. Nina had once seen it hanging in her mother's closet, stuck between a gold lamé pantsuit that Ida had snatched from the jaws of her building's trash compactor and a very old and very ugly op-art bathrobe. Nina had pulled the three offending garments off their hangers and shook them in her mother's face. "Lamé?" she had shrieked. "When in God's name are you ever going to wear lamé?"

"Velour came back," Ida had snapped.

"Velour is not lamé," Nina had retorted.

Now Ida reinserted her plastic bag of ice in her freezer, then sat down. "How was the flight?" she asked.

"Okay." Nina sat down in the chair across from her. "But tell me something."

"What?"

"There's one thing I just don't understand. You're out of town, in an airport—L.A., Pittsburgh, wherever. And you're sitting on the toilet and you need some toilet paper. The roll's there, you pull some out, transaction completed, right? But then you hit LaGuardia and it's a whole different story. Even if the paper's there, you can't get any momentum going when you try to roll. You've got to pull it off piece by piece. Now, how could it be that toilet paper will only roll out of town? Can you tell me how this could be possible?"

"A minor irritation." Ida waved her hand dismissively. "Compared to the real burning issue."

"Which is?"

"The fact that women in New York pee all over the seat. When you're out of town, you can at least sit down on a toilet without doing a mop-up operation first."

"It's true, isn't it." Nina sat thoughtfully for a few moments. "I've chosen to return to the only city in the country where every toilet seat is a land mine."

"Why *did* you come back?" Ida's voice wasn't harsh exactly, but it was straightforward. "I knew you weren't particularly happy; I could tell by your phone calls. But I thought it was just, you know, the usual."

"It was worse than that. I guess I didn't want to kvetch at long-distance rates. But I was going under. Believe me, I tried. You think I want to start all over again at forty? In this market? No apartments, no jobs, no husbands. You know I wouldn't have done it if I hadn't really needed to."

"But why? What happened? Was it Jonathan?"

"Oh, he was all right. Nice enough, not horrible to me or anything, pretty much the same as when we lived here. But he was mostly thinking about his job, so distracted, not really listening to anything I was saying. That petit mal syndrome men have. Their eyes glaze over when you use compound sentences. You know what I mean?"

"Yeah. Your father wasn't too bad, actually. I used to come home from school all pent up with complaints about the assistant principal and he'd hang in there with me for quite some time."

"Well, you always told a pretty good story. I don't know, maybe I'm losing my narrative line."

"Don't be silly, Nina. The guy's transferred to a new office, it's a company that loves to lay people off. He's nervous, he's distracted. It's natural, it has nothing to do with you."

"I guess. But it wasn't really Jonathan. He wasn't the reason I left. It was the way people looked at me."

"And how did they look at you?"

"Like I was a specimen. Of a certain type. They'd peruse me for a minute, just to diagnose me. Like they were a lepidopterist and I was a dead butterfly. And then recognition would dawn and I could almost hear them telling themselves, 'Oh, yeah, I've seen one of those before. She's one of those New York Jewish women. Damn feisty critters they are. Loud, too. Give you a right powerful headache.'" Somewhere in the middle of her speech, Nina had acquired a Kentucky twang.

"Oh, that's ridiculous. This is Los Angeles we're talking about, not the Ozarks. California is filled with Jews."

"The men do better than the women. Nobody ever gave Jonathan one of those butterfly looks and then immediately started talking about how much they hate Barbra Streisand."

"You're being paranoid."

"Maybe." *Just because you're paranoid doesn't mean that no one's out to get you.* Kids had said it in the fourth grade and it had turned out to be true. Well, if Nina was going to be paranoid, she was going to be paranoid in New York City where it was still the local pastime.

"By the way, Laura called to ask if you want to go to a funeral with them tomorrow."

"Whose funeral?"

"A friend of Ken's. Someone he went to college with. Laura says you knew him. Andy somebody."

"Andy Campbell? That guy who does research at Morgan?"

"I think so."

"They fixed me up with him, before he was married."

"And?"

"And nothing. But how did he die? He was my age."

"I'm not sure. They did do an autopsy. Laura was sort of vague about it. But I got the impression that he didn't die a completely natural death."

Nina tried to picture Andy Campbell as the victim of foul play. It seemed unlikely. He had radiated wholesomeness. Nina remembered sitting across a table from him, in some fish place in the Village, listening to him talk about transplanting a mosquito ovary. Nina had been tempted to call an end to the evening's festivities right in the middle of his entomological soliloquy. Not because he was excruciatingly boring, which he was, but because he seemed so simple, so focused. She knew that if they had ever gotten married, she would spend the rest of her life listening to him say "Nina, what are you making such a big deal about?"

He had grown up on an upstate dairy farm and met Ken, Nina's brother-in-law, when they were both undergraduates at Cornell's School of Agriculture. Ken went on to medical school while Andy got a Ph.D. in public health. Why he had come to New York City was a mystery whose solution had eluded Nina. "Why did he bother?" she asked Laura after the Jane Street date. "He's the kind of guy who would be happier anywhere else. Why would he choose to put up with this shit if he doesn't have to?"

"He's got a very big grant," Laura had said. "According to Ken, people would kill to get into his department at Morgan University. Supposedly he's very brilliant."

"Well, he didn't get his doctorate in dinner conversation, that I can tell you."

"Nina." The two syllables conveyed a paragraph, which ran something like: "You can continue to be picky. That's your prerogative. But you've got to be prepared to take the consequences. Which means living alone for the rest of your life in a drafty, leaky dump."

What Laura never understood was that Nina being picky wasn't the problem. That was just the convenient explanation. In any event, Andy Campbell was the last person you'd expect to find dead, much less murdered. It was easier to picture him growing old behind his microscope, his collections of specimens increasing to the point of crowding him out.

"What do you mean when you say that he didn't die a completely natural death?" she asked Ida.

"I don't know. I'm just repeating what Laura told me."

"Hmmm. Interesting. So, shall we go to the funeral?"

"Are you kidding? I never even met the guy. Do you think I'm one of those ghoulish old ladies who haunts funeral parlors?"

"What time is it scheduled for?"

"Two, I think. You're going to have to get a job eventually. You know that, don't you?"

Nina sighed. "I know." But for the moment, schnorrering off of her widowed, pensioned mother, running off to whatever midday funeral caught her fancy, didn't seem to be such a bad life.

CHAPTER THREE

"**OF COURSE YOU SHOULD COME,**" Laura said when Nina called the next morning.

"But I hardly knew the guy. Why should I go to his funeral?"

"It's not a funeral. It's just a memorial service in his house. Andy would have appreciated it. He liked you, Nina. He always asked about you. He thought you were really smart and funny."

Smart and *funny* were fighting words. Up there with *such a pretty face.* No one ever said such things about thin women.

"Well, where did he live?"

"In Park Slope. Over on Thirteenth Street. You can come here and see the kids afterward."

"Thirteenth Street, huh?" Park Slope streets had either numbers or names. Names were better, and the lower the number the classier the address. Thirteenth Street was not the kind of place where people had stripped all their molding. "What's the wife's name?"

"Roz. Roz Brillstein. She uses her own name."

"How is she handling it?"

"Okay, I think. She's a tough cookie. Very tied to her mother. Andy always felt like an outsider."

"You mean she'll hardly notice that he's gone?"

"No, nothing like that. Believe me, you've got two kids, you'll notice if your husband dies."

Laura snapped just enough to make Nina feel like a self-absorbed jerk with a limited comprehension of normal human emotions. Something was wrong when she had to actively try to remember that someone's husband and father had just died. That Andy Campbell had been more than a failed blind date.

"But I think," Laura continued, "that Mrs. Brillstein will help her to . . . um . . . absorb the loss, if you know what I mean."

Nina tried to picture the kind of woman Andy Campbell might have married. Who would he have been happy with? A quiet, modest woman with great powers of concentration, like himself, with a love of the outdoors. A polar-fleece, mountain-bike sort of woman. "What does Roz look like?" Nina asked.

"Sort of flashy, in a way."

"I can't picture Andy with someone flashy. Even the chamois shirt he wore on our date was beige."

"They were an unusual couple. But Roz is so unusual that she'd be part of an unusual couple no matter who she married."

"What's so unusual about her?"

"It's hard to describe. You'd have to meet her in person in order to picture it." Laura paused, then continued. "She was born in Europe, right after the war, in a displaced-persons camp. The parents are Polish. Actually, her father died not too long ago."

"And she's a flashy child of the Holocaust?"

"Well, the Brillsteins were furriers. And they doted on Roz, always making her little fur capes with matching muffs when she was a kid, stuff like that. So she has sort of an old-world elegance that she kinda pulls off. Although sometimes it gets a little ridiculous, like when she tried to play tennis in her sandals when they were out at our beach house for the weekend. You occasionally feel like screaming at her to just get a pair of sneakers already. But most of the time it works."

"What does she do for a living?"

"She's a custom milliner."

"No shit." Nina suddenly realized that of course she was going to attend Andy Campbell's memorial service. That she was already hooked, and couldn't possibly pass up a chance to take a look at Roz Brillstein. Besides, it made Nina feel better that even though she had only been in New York for twelve hours, she already had something to do. Even if it was something morbid, at least it was a scheduled activity. During her months in Los Angeles, the only scheduled activity she had managed to come up with was taking in the newspaper.

"So Mom said something about an autopsy. What's the story?" Nina asked.

"The official word is that he had a sudden aneurysm. That's what it said in the *Times* obit. But Roz told Ken that something turned up in his blood."

"Something? Something like what? Like poison?"

"Yeah."

"Yeah, like poison?"

"Yeah, like poison."

"What kind of poison?"

"What's the difference?" Laura always had little patience for Nina's mental meandering. It was clear that she thought her sister had too much time on her hands.

"Well, wouldn't you like to know how he was poisoned?" Nina asked.

"So that I could picture Andy dropping dead more clearly? No, I don't think so. Anyway, are you coming this afternoon? Because if you are, you'd better write down the address."

"I'm not walking in there myself," Nina said. "I'll pick you up at your house and go with you."

"But the F train's much closer. Coming all the way over here first is totally out of your way."

"I have no way." It was an overstatement, but being single, unemployed, and homeless came pretty close.

CHAPTER
FOUR

THE BRILLSTEIN-CAMPBELL HOUSE had only the thinnest veneer of Victoriana about it. Unlike the brownstone that Laura and Ken had carefully restored, Roz's house exuded an air of drama that began with the black wreath on the front door.

"Look at that." Nina pointed to the intricate construction of black lace, ribbons, and spray-painted twigs.

"Roz's handiwork, no doubt," Laura said.

"You think so?"

"Absolutely," said Ken. "Paint the whole thing white, rotate it ninety degrees, and it would look great on the head of a bride, don't you think?"

"You mean to tell me that the first thing this woman does when she finds out that her husband's been killed is sit down and start painting a pile of twigs black?"

"No," said Ken, "I think she glued them together first."

"Don't be ridiculous," Laura said. "Roz is the designer. She doesn't actually sit down and do the handiwork."

"So who does?"

"She's got a bunch of Ecuadoreans."

"Of course," Nina said. "I should have known. Where does she keep them?"

"Upstairs. I don't mean that they live up there. That's

where she has her business. On the top floor of the
house."

"After all, why waste the garden level on a bunch of
Ecuadoreans?" Nina snapped. "Stick 'em up on top,
where the ceilings are low. They're short, they won't notice."

"Roz isn't like that," Laura said. "She's impossible to
hate, even though you might want to. Believe me, I've
tried."

"I'll try harder."

"No, wait. You'll see what I mean." Laura knocked on
the door.

A small old woman in a big black hat opened the door.
She wore a simple gray wool suit that looked like it had
been purchased before Arnold Constable closed its doors.
The hat, while not quite as intricate as the wreath on the
door, seemed to have been constructed by the same
hand.

"Mrs. Brillstein." Laura leaned down and gave her a
kiss on the cheek. "We're all so sorry about Andy. Such a
terrible thing."

"Yes, it is. After all I've seen in my life, I never thought
I'd have to see this." The accent was strong.

"I know, I can't believe it. Mrs. Brillstein, you've met
my husband, Ken, before, haven't you?"

"I think so, yes."

"And this is my sister, Nina. She knew Andy."

Mrs. Brillstein nodded toward Nina. The woman somehow managed to take in every detail without actually
looking her up and down. Nina knew that the salt stains
on her suede boots and the dirt on the hem of her coat
had all been duly noted by Mrs. Brillstein without so
much as a downward glance. "Do you know my daughter?" she asked Nina.

"Um, no." Why did it feel like she was confessing to

something? She had never even slept with Andy. At least, she was pretty sure she hadn't. After twenty years of dating, you sometimes get confused about these things.

"Come with me." Mrs. Brillstein led them over to a coatrack that had been set up in the front hall. "Please hang up your coats."

Nina craned her neck slightly so that she could see past the coats, around into the living room. The *parlor*, she supposed, was the preferred term in this part of Brooklyn. But the room had no parlorish characteristics. The moldings had all been removed, the ceiling plastered over to abolish any hint of corbel. The walls were painted dead white and lined with oversize canvases.

The paintings all seemed to be by the same artist. Whoever the painter was, he or she had probably been quite taken with Georgia O'Keeffe at the time the oils were executed, since they featured large, colorful forms that might represent flowers but could just as easily represent vaginas. For a moment Nina thought she might have wandered into an art gallery, since the furniture was sparse and people stood around in small knots, sipping white wine. But then Roz Brillstein herself came sweeping down upon them to remind everyone of the sober nature of the occasion.

"Laura, Ken, thank you so much for coming." Roz Brillstein was a swirl of fabric, all in different textures, varying in color from inky blue to jet-black. Nina couldn't quite discern where one garment began and another ended. There were so many of them—a blouse and a vest and a jacket and a long skirt. And a hat, of course. It was more of a veil, actually, than a hat. A bit of black netting propped up by a black wooden comb inlaid with squares of mother-of-pearl. The veil reached just to the tip of her nose, so Roz Brillstein didn't need to lift it up in order to kiss Ken and Laura on their cheeks.

"And you must be Nina." Roz turned and whooshed her clothing in Nina's direction. Nina again felt her salt stains being perused. Fighting fire with fire, Nina checked out the Brillstein ensemble.

Don't wear navy with black, the magazines cautioned. But the advice had nothing to do with what Roz had assembled. The blouse was high-necked, mock Victorian, shiny dark silk with tiny black pearl buttons all the way up. The vest was boxy and long, fashioned out of some kind of dotted swiss rayon in a midnight blue. It also had pearl buttons, but only three oversize ones—which were sort of pinkish, as if they'd come from the inside of a conch shell.

The jacket, on the other hand, had no buttons. And it was really more of a coat than a jacket, since it reached past Roz Brillstein's knees. It had East Ninth Street written all over it, sold in the kind of store that also offers African thumb pianos and rainsticks. The material was a patchwork quilt made of fabrics that, for the most part, were highly textured. Puckers, tufts, and nubbiness abounded. The colors were inky, sometimes drifting off into a steely blue or a violet-gray. Underneath the jacket was a long trumpet skirt made out of a thick-cut velvet and a pair of high-heeled black suede boots that laced up the front.

In contrast to the yards of dark fabric, Roz's face looked like a small porcelain teacup perched on a mound of coal. It was a delicate face, very white, with large dark eyes burning through. Her hair, which probably at one time had been the same brown as her eyes, was chemically burnished to a deep burgundy. It was extremely thick, shaped into a chin-length wedge that stood out inches from her neck.

Roz's neck was short and thick and her shoulders were wide. It took Nina several minutes to realize that Roz

Brillstein was actually quite stubby. Five feet two inches at the most and probably at least one hundred and fifty pounds. Stubbiness was not, however, one of the first things you thought of when you looked at her.

The entire effect, which easily could have been completely *schmattadicheh*, was actually quite elegant. Roz Brillstein didn't need a swanlike neck to make you feel like you were talking to a woman of aristocratic bearing. True, the aristocracy might have been totally self-contained in a small Polish shtetl, but the posture was erect and the manners impeccable.

"It's so nice to meet you." Roz put a small hand on Nina's forearm. Nina half expected it to be encased in a black lace glove. But there it was, naked except for its pearly, translucent coat of nail polish.

"Listen, I'm so sorry about Andy," Nina said, while Roz's hand remained on her arm. "I mean, it's so awful. I sort of knew him. Uh, I hadn't seen him in a long time, of course, but, you know, he was a really great guy."

Roz just stood there perfectly still, her hand resting on Nina's arm as if it were the most natural thing. She looked off into the distance, through her front hall and up her stairway. She half smiled and Nina mentally scrambled to decipher the smile. If only they made smile decipherers, like those machines that could take a gallon of paint and break it down into its components. Roz's smile seemed wistful, but also smug and provocative. Nina wondered what a smile like that could mean.

"Andrew." Roz dilated her nostrils as she sharply exhaled. "He was my husband. How will I ever go on without him?" She withdrew her hand and posed with both hands folded, as if reciting haiku. Nina went back and counted. Yup, seventeen syllables exactly. Very impressive.

"How are the kids doing?" Laura asked.

"Well, Shoshi seems to be pretty calm. But Wolf is still absolutely hysterical."

Could it be true? Could this woman have actually named her son Wolf? At least Nina hoped it was a boy. If she had named her daughter Wolf, the kid had better be damn good-looking.

Nina tried to imagine what the mixing of the Brillstein and Campbell genes would produce. It was hard to remember exactly what Andy had looked like. It was so easy to dismiss him as a type—a tall, blond, small-nosed ectomorph. But now that she thought about it, his nose had not really been small. It had been largish, certainly bigger than the beautiful Grecian specimen perched on Roz's porcelain face.

Had Roz's been altered? These days it was harder to tell. Rhinoplasters had learned a thing or two since Dr. Diamond had taken a scalpel to his first Jewish proboscis. These days they did tricks, things like leaving little bumps to throw you off the track.

It would be interesting to see the children that Roz and Andy had produced. Even if they hadn't been on the opposite ends of the spectrum in coloring, height, and ethnicity, their temperaments were so different that it was hard to imagine the two of them forming a family unit. Roz exuded drama out of every pore, not to mention out of every accessory. Andy had been your prototypical scientist, calm and rational to the point where you could just scream.

Nina looked around the room in an attempt to locate one of their progeny. The first thing that stood out, however, was the textured fabrics. In an extension of the tendencies she exhibited while getting dressed, Roz had liberally padded the room with kilim pillows, piano shawls, embroidered antimacassars, and lots of patterned rugs. The woman had a fabric fetish. The furniture, however, was simple and untextured—two brown leather Barcelona chairs and an oversize couch covered in beige wool.

On one of the Barcelona chairs sprawled a boy, maybe eight years old, kicking his shoe against a chrome chair leg. Was this Wolf? If so, he had his mother's eyes, darkly luminous in a pale face. His clothing looked handmade, a matching vest and pants in a charcoal velour over a red turtleneck. His shoes were red suede and they laced up the side. Very cool, but a little androgynous. How hard it must be to be named Wolf *and* have your shoes lace up the side.

Nina looked around for Shoshi. There was a group of little girls in the dining room, but none of them particularly stood out. The dining room table was simple, almost Shaker, in a dark stained cherry. The chairs were postwar Eames, in a 1952 shade of blond. On the table were baskets of breads, cheeses, and crudités. The baskets looked suspiciously like hats with handles.

Roz turned to greet a frail, elderly couple that was slowly shuffling toward her. "Anka, Roman, how are you?" She swooped down to hug them. The woman had a gray bun and wore a suit of an even earlier vintage than Mrs. Brillstein's. Actually, the suit looked sort of familiar. Was Nina imagining things or had her Barbie doll once owned the same suit? Or maybe it was something that Jackie Kennedy had worn in a televised tour of the White House and it looked different without the pillbox. My God, they had cut the armholes so tight back then. Nina made a mental note to give thanks for loose armholes when she sat down at the Thanksgiving table next month.

Since Roz seemed occupied and Laura and Ken had become absorbed in conversation with a woman wearing an outfit that matched her child's, Nina let herself drift over to the food. There were buried treasures among the baskets of baby carrots and water crackers. A Mexican bowl held a healthy supply of those adorable little marinated mozzarella balls. Nina always found them sweet, tenderly nestled among butchered bits of sundried tomatoes. To make them even more appealing, next to the bowl someone had placed one of those etched crystal shot glasses that Nina's grandfather used to drink schnapps out of. Propped up in the shot glass were these adorable little forks with Bakelite handles. Roz Brillstein was full of surprises.

Nina picked up a Bakelite fork and speared a mozzarella ball. What was she doing here anyway? It had been stupid to come, almost ghoulish. Was she that starved for cheese and company? She sat down in an Eames chair and leaned back to eavesdrop on the closest available conversation. She lowered her eyes and tuned in.

"I can't believe he didn't come," an Asian woman in black slacks and a red vest was saying.

"He said he had to go out of town for a couple of days." The speaker was a guy with curly hair and glasses, in a maroon crewneck Shetland sweater.

"Where did he go?"

"I don't know. He wouldn't say."

"I heard he went to northern California, for a tour of some wine company." The woman delicately nibbled one of the mozzarella balls.

"Oh, nice. Ever been?"

"No. Chinese women aren't known for being wine connoisseurs, you know."

"You could learn. Jewish men never used to know anything about alcohol and now some of them write wine columns for very prestigious periodicals."

"Yes, I've heard that they've become some of the most pretentious oenophiles in the country."

"Oh." He didn't look offended, but he didn't look amused either. "Want some caponata?" he asked.

"I'll pass, thanks."

"Okay." He stepped over and spooned a pile of caponata onto his plate.

"So what time did you get out of the lab last night?"

"Oh, God, it must have been past midnight. If I never see another small furry vagina, I'd be a happy man."

"Oh, come on, David. Guinea pig genitalia is your life. You know that."

"Sometimes it feels that way."

"Friends." A voice rose above the general din of sympathetic murmurs and the click of Bakelite forks on Mexican pottery. It was Roz. "Friends," she repeated, opening her arms, "thank you all for coming. You can't imagine how much it means to me." Her voice was as dark and rich as a chocolate soufflé. If she ever got sick of the hat biz, Roz could do well as a rabbi, as long as the congregation was into funky clothes.

"I'd like to take this opportunity to say a few words in memory of my beloved Andrew. When I'm through, I'd welcome any of you who would like to join in with thoughts or memories."

Nina stood up and faced Roz. The guinea pig gynecologist put down his caponata. Laura broke off her conversation with the young mom in the flowered jumper. Everyone stood at attention while Roz let loose.

CHAPTER FIVE

HALF AN HOUR LATER there wasn't a dry eye in the house. Roz had run through Andy Campbell's childhood on the dairy farm, his discovery of microbiology at the Cornell School of Agriculture, his meteoric rise as a research scientist, and his ultimate fulfillment when he met Roz Brillstein, his one true love.

"Where are his parents?" Nina whispered to Laura as they both blew their noses into the tissues that Roz had tastefully and discreetly provided in each corner of the room.

"The Campbells? Oh, Roz wouldn't have invited them."

"Why not?"

"As the casting director of the Roz Brillstein show, she just couldn't find a part for them."

"How did she get away with that?"

"I'll explain after we get ourselves out of here," Laura said.

"I don't know why, but I don't think I'm quite ready to leave yet." Nina couldn't explain the feeling, but it had something to do with not being able to tear herself away from Roz.

"I know, I know. It's Roz. On some level, she makes you sick. But you can't get enough of her, right?"

"Exactly. Like the old joke about the hotel in the Cats-kills. Such terrible food. And such small portions."

Laura nodded. "That's Roz. Come on, let's say our good-byes."

"Where's Ken?"

"Oh, he already left. Didn't you see him in the corner on his portable phone? I would have been embarrassed, but I don't think Roz noticed."

"I bet Mrs. Brillstein did."

After a tearful farewell from Roz and another once-over from Mrs. Brillstein, Nina finally found herself on the street listening to Laura's dissection of the dynamics of the Brillstein-Campbell clan.

"Roz would never have invited the Campbells," Laura said, "because as far as she was concerned, they didn't really exist."

"You mean that she wasn't talking to them?"

"No, nothing as obvious as that. If she found herself in the same room with them, she'd be as charming as hell. But she'd never mention them, never call them, never invite them over, never take them into account."

"And how did Andy deal with that?" Nina asked.

"I guess he managed to maintain some kind of inde-pendent relationship with them. I don't know—most men aren't good at that sort of thing."

"You mean like Daddy's famous line when he'd pick up the telephone? 'Ida, it's for you, it's my mother.' "

"Exactly. So it was easy for Roz to elbow Andy's par-ents out of the family."

"And they must have felt a natural tendency to steer clear of her."

"Yeah, they're not exactly pushy people to begin with."

"I can imagine. Roz would probably scare the shit out of almost any dairy farmer, don't you think?"

"They just didn't know what to make of her," Laura said. "For one thing, she was practically their age."

"No shit!"

"Well, not really. But she was quite a bit older than Andy."

"And how old was he?"

"He was in Ken's class at Cornell. That's how they met. So that would make him almost forty."

"And Roz?"

"God knows she wouldn't tell anyone. But she loves to talk about how she was born in a displaced persons camp in Germany. Now, I don't know exactly how long after the war they kept those things going. But my guess is that Roz is definitely somewhere in the last trimester of her forties. She looks good, don't you think? Great skin."

"I guess so. I was so busy looking at the veil and the velvet and the suede and the Bakelite, I didn't spend too much time on her skin."

"She's got some Romanian who sells her special herb soaks or something."

"I'm sure she does," Nina said. "How ever did they meet?"

"Who? Roz and the Romanian?"

"Roz and Andy."

"He was dating her roommate."

"I can't picture Roz with a roommate. She takes up so much space. More so metaphorically than physically. She's larger than life."

"Well, she had a long series of roommates. Roz had a great apartment on the Lower East Side, but no one lasted."

"She kicked them all out?"

"No, they'd eventually leave. Roz would throw their saffron into her rice, pour their imported bath salts into her tub, stuff like that."

"And this last one? She just snatched up her boy-friend?"

"Yeah, I guess Roz can be quite a drain."

"She sounds more like a siphon."

Laura laughed. Nina recognized the laugh as her own. All the Fischman women had the same laugh, a short bark used sparingly. No trilling, no tinkling, nothing from the belly. Just a short, monosyllabic "ha," an acknowledgment that a joke had been made and that it passed muster.

Humor in the Fischman household had been the basic form of currency, the only deck the family had to play with. This had been true in many Bronx households, and the boroughs of New York City had somehow become the spawning ground of professionals and hobbyists.

When the family is in the business, so to speak, one achieves a casual fluency, an intimate use of the language that allows you never to raise your voice. So when a bunch of old-time comics get together for dinner or pinochle at the Friars' Club, most jokes are acknowledged by mere nods or raised eyebrows. The Fischmans did not belong to the Friars, so they let themselves emit a syllable of vocal acknowledgment, but not much more.

The women had been trained well by Leo Fischman. In the traditional Jewish family, humor was part of the male domain. More so than money. The common misconception is that Jewish men were good with money, while the truth is that back in the shtetl, the man was busy wasting the day in shul while the wife ran the store.

But humor was something else. Humor was a realm where the women had to sit upstairs. In fact, Jewish women often prided themselves on a certain air of humorlessness. They cultivated their naïveté before marriage and a grim hardheadedness afterward.

Nina had always felt that the true test of feminism was

not going to law school or taking a female lover, but rather the grit and determination to take a thought and wring every possible bit of humor from it. And then force it down people's throats. The truly liberated Jewish woman not only picked up her own check, but also made her own jokes.

It amazed her how many otherwise assertive women backed away from humor, even in New York, possibly the humor capital of the world. They acted as if it were some sort of complicated stick shift that they just couldn't manage.

Leo Fischman had been egalitarian about humor. Perhaps if he had had a son, he would have invested more in him. But Leo was surrounded by women, ones with potential for that sort of thing, and he let Ida step right up and be the funny one. And his daughters were encouraged to tell their fledgling little jokes at the dinner table for practice, so they could get stronger. As if they were learning to ice-skate and had to build up their ankle muscles.

Laura's almost silent acknowledgment of Nina's joke, the one about Roz being more of a siphon than a drain, served as a reminder. For Nina tended to forget that she and Laura had started out from the same place. That they were *landsleit*, in effect, though they had fared differently on the foreign soil of adulthood.

"So what do you think happened to Andy?" Nina asked.

"You mean do I think that Roz did him in?"

"I didn't mean that specifically, but since you brought it up, *do* you think Roz did him in?"

"Umm, I guess it's possible. She can be sort of scary sometimes."

"What about Mrs. Brillstein? She was really scary," Nina said.

"You think that woman schlepped herself through the Holocaust and made a new life in Queens just so she could kill the father of her grandchildren?"

"Is that kid's name really Wolf?"

"Yeah, he was named after Mrs. Brillstein's brother who didn't make it through."

"I wouldn't want to trade places with that child. As if he didn't have a hard enough time with a name like Wolf and a mother like Roz. Now this had to happen."

"I know," Laura said. "Andy provided a lot of stability in the family. Roz has a high sense of drama. For someone who runs a small millinery business out of her house, she has a lot of business crises."

"A millinery business. So old-fashioned."

"The family were furriers. That's how Roz started with hats. She'd take the fur scraps that her parents were going to throw away and use them to trim the hats she'd crochet."

"Where's Mr. Brillstein?"

"He died last year. But he kept the business going up until the end. Even though he was making mostly novelty items by that time."

"Like what?"

"Bunny rabbit slippers and fox-trimmed bathrobes. It seems that people will only wear fur someplace where no one can see."

"So Roz makes hats." Nina was always impressed by how many women had successfully schemed their way out of going to law school. A law degree seemed like one big sand trap that was there waiting for you if you didn't watch out. For a brief moment Nina pictured herself as a milliner, fastening a spray of silk roses to a cloche. She doubted whether she'd be successful, since she had a hard time even pulling her pantyhose on straight.

"Yes, Roz makes hats. She'll also make you a little collar that matches, to pin on your sweater or coat."

Nina had a sudden thought. "My God," she said, "what are they going to do for money? I hope Andy was overinsured. Even on the wrong side of Park Slope, the mortgage of a brownstone must be beyond the reach of a hatmaker."

"Milliner."

"Whatever."

"He was carrying a lot of life insurance."

"How do you know?"

"I just know," Laura said. "It's the kind of thing people talk about with each other. I could probably run down the entire list of our friends and tell you who's underinsured and who's not."

"Must make for fun dinner parties." Is that what Nina wanted? To be married and sit around with a bunch of other couples and discuss life insurance policies? It made being single look good. If only she could eliminate dating from her schedule, her life might not be too bad.

Maybe that was the way to go. Stop dating. Stop working. Move in with your mother. Stay up late watching *Letterman*, then spend the day attending memorial services for people you don't really know. It occurred to Nina that she was in the process of successfully re-creating the life of an adult schizophrenic, but without all the bother of having a mental illness.

All those years of schlepping briefcases and running to the dry cleaners and setting alarm clocks. And looking with envy at people sitting in coffee shops wearing jeans and reading the want ads. Now here she was. Who ever thought she'd be so privileged?

She would, however, have to schedule some activities a little more upbeat than memorial services. She didn't want to repeat her last New York unemployed period, while she was waiting for the bar exam results, when she spent three months sitting in the lobby of the Museum of Modern Art, listening to the conversations of people she didn't know but who were wearing clothing and talking about things that Nina couldn't afford. Eavesdropping could be a creative and stimulating activity, but it should be something you did on the side, not the main activity of your day.

"So where are you off to now?" asked Laura as they headed down Seventh Avenue.

"Um, I don't know." Nina scared herself with her answer. It was true that she had sat around like a lox in L.A. for months. But back home, she always had someplace she was off to—the office, court, the gym, the shrink, and on and on. Now here she was with no place to be off to. She could always re-up at the gym and at the shrink. But until she found a job, she didn't think that either renewal was financially advisable.

For that matter, she could probably crawl back to her old office and convince them to reinstate her. But the thought was so unbearable that she put it out of her mind.

"Why don't you come up for a cup of tea," Laura suggested.

Laura and her goddamn tea. Five different kinds of zingers, little bunny rabbit mugs, and a Winnie-the-Pooh honey dispenser. The wind picked up and swept down on them from Prospect Park. Nina pulled her collar up against her ears.

"Do you have any orange zinger?" she asked her sister.

"Sure."

"Well then, I can't think of anything I'd like better than a nice hot cup of tea."

CHAPTER
SIX

AS LONG AS SHE WAS PUTTING honey into her orange zinger, Nina figured that she might as well have a piece of zucchini bread on the side. It was the type of baked good that had positive memories for Nina. Memories of living off-campus in a big old house with a lot of roommates and dogs and packets of ZigZag rolling papers all over the place.

Laura served the zucchini bread on a cake plate trimmed with little red hearts, but at least the teacup was devoid of any cutesy decoration. Nina's sister grabbed a healthy slice for herself and sat down at the kitchen table. That was one of the good things about her. She might have Laura Ashley tea cozies and a teapot in the shape of a duck, but at least she ate. Being thin was more forgivable if it was something that just happened to you, without any prearrangement.

"You know what I'm really worried about?" she said to Nina.

"What's that?"

"Our real estate investments."

"What's the matter? Running out of money?"

"No, we're okay. But Ken put some money in this real estate investment with Andy. Something that Roz's father had set up. Andy and Ken were equal partners. Now we're going to have to deal with Roz. Do you have any idea what that's going to be like?"

"I can imagine," said Nina. "What does Ken think?"

"I haven't discussed it with him. Umm, I don't think he even knows that I know about the building."

"What do you mean?" Nina finished her zucchini bread and resisted pressing her fingers into the remaining crumbs.

"Well, I pieced together most of this, so I'm not sure of what's true and what's not. But as far as I can tell, what happened was that Mr. Brillstein and his friend owned an apartment house in Borough Park. They were both getting very old and Mr. Brillstein's friend needed cash. He didn't have any children, so Roz's father agreed to find somebody to buy the friend out while Mr. Brillstein gave his half to Andy."

"Very sexist."

"Well, not really. Maybe part of it was that he was old-world about these things. But there was also a problem, since Roz was a total disaster when it came to finances. She had defaulted on her student loans, was on a payment plan with the IRS, and almost declared personal bankruptcy so many times that I think even she lost count. You know what she ended up doing with all of her credit cards?"

"Cut them up?"

"No, she couldn't quite bring herself to get rid of them permanently. So she used to freeze them in a big block of ice. And if she still wanted to make the purchase once they thawed, she'd go ahead and buy it."

"What a great idea."

"I could see why her father wouldn't want the building in her name," Laura said. "Every time she'd get a notice of any violation, she'd be down at the buildings depart-

ment screaming bloody murder as if she were making a
return at Bloomingdale's."

"Yeah, real estate is a tough business. If you've got a
penchant for histrionics, you can really do a lot of dam-
age. The successful landlords that I deal with . . . uh,
that I used to deal with have nerves of steel. A lot of them
are Holocaust survivors. I guess they figure if they got
through that, they can get through anything."

"Yeah, well, Mr. Brillstein was exactly like that. And
Andy, as a scientist, really had the same kind of dispas-
sionate detachment."

"So in a way," Nina said, "Roz married her father after
all. Even though one was raised in a shtetl and the other
grew up on a dairy farm."

"You know, you're right. I never thought of it that way
before. Anyhow, Mr. Brillstein knew that if Roz had anything to do with the building, it would mean disaster. So
he put the deed in Andy's name, even though he would
have preferred not to. And then Andy talked Ken into
buying the other half, but Ken never told me because he
knew I would split a gut."

"Why?"

"Who needs the aggravation of owning rental property
in New York City? Is that why he went to medical school?
To be a landlord?"

"So how come you let him do it?"

"I only found out about it afterward, when it was already too late."

"How'd you find out?"

Laura carried the plates over to the sink. Nina realized
that the hearts on the dishes matched the hearts on the
tiles that made up the backsplash behind the sink.

"One day," Laura said, "the managing agent called. It
was some emergency and he couldn't get a hold of Ken or
Andy. He said there was trouble at the building. So I

asked him what building he was talking about and he told me."

"And you never confronted Ken?"

"No, I never mentioned it to him."

"I don't get it. Are you intimidated by him because he earns all the money? You could get a job, you know."

Laura looked Nina straight in the eye. "I like things the way they are," she said. "And as far as confronting him about this building in Borough Park goes . . . well, why should I? Do I really want to know about broken pipes and posted violations and deadbeat tenants?"

"No, but you hear all these stories about wives who keep their heads in the sand while everything is going to ruin around them."

"Do you honestly feel that my monitoring this situation is going to help matters at all?"

"But isn't that like saying there's no point in having a mammogram?" asked Nina.

"No, it's different. If they find a lump, I'll go see an oncologist. If Ken tells me that the roof needs to be replaced, what am I going to do about it? Quite frankly, I'd rather not know."

She'd rather not know. As simple as that. Nina wondered if she would ever be able to say that about anything other than her weight.

"So," Laura asked, "how long are you going to be staying with Mom?"

Good question. It depended on how long it would take to reestablish her life. To find a nice, cheap, well-located apartment in Manhattan. To find a fun law job that paid well and didn't require working ridiculous hours. Simple things like that. "Probably forever," Nina said.

"Get out of here. I give it two weeks."

"And where am I supposed to go?"

"I know someone looking for a live-in. Two sons, ages three and six. A thousand a month."

"Do I get to sleep with the husband?"

"I don't think you'll be tempted."

"Yeah, I know. I just dumped the last decent available man in the United States."

"Good move. I must say, I was rather surprised to hear of your sudden return."

"California was so awful."

"Remember, you're talking to someone whose husband did his residency in Scottsdale."

"Yeah, that place probably makes Los Angeles look like West End Avenue."

"It was pretty bad," Laura said. "But Ken got a lot of practice treating melanoma."

"Arizona must be the melanoma capital of the world."

"No, actually Australia is."

"Australia probably makes Scottsdale look like West End Avenue." Nina flung her hand to cut herself off. "Enough. You win. You're more flexible than I am."

"Well, I had age going for me. How old was I when we went out to Arizona? No more than twenty-five. When you're that young you can do anything. Forty is a different story."

"Are you implying that I've become ossified?"

"That might be an appropriate word."

"*Ossified*? No," said Nina. "I'm worse than ossified. I'm petrified."

"What are you so scared of?"

"A clinical depression."

"Okay." Laura turned her attention to wiping off the kitchen counter.

It worried Nina that her sister had no snappy retort for her. Why hadn't she come back with "Nina, you? A clinical depression? Out of the question." Nina hated the thought of being depressed. She couldn't help but hope for something more upbeat and creative, like a multiple personality or at least bipolar disorder.

Years ago, when she was just out of law school, *The New Yorker* had run a series of articles about an interesting and imaginative young schizophrenic named Sylvia Frumkin. Susan Sheehan's series had been devoured by Nina and her friends. Much discussion had been devoted to similarities between themselves and Sylvia. For years afterward, whenever one of them exhibited any type of bizarre behavior, they would point at each other and scream "Sylvia Frumkin."

Well, Sylvia Frumkin was dead, according to a recent update in *The New Yorker*. She had died an ignoble death on the floor of the Rockland Psychiatric Center and there had been nothing upbeat or creative about it. As it turned out, you needed all the sanity you could muster to get by in the world. Nina was sure that the latest crop of female law graduates were not spending their off-hours empathizing with any schizophrenic, no matter how charming she might be.

And Laura was apparently unwilling to be reassuring about Nina's hints at a clinical depression. Mental illness was not something you wanted anywhere near your family these days, when everyone already felt like they were hanging by a thread.

"By the way, where are the kids?" Nina asked.

"Danielle's at Hebrew school. She'll be back at five. Jared's playing soccer and I think he's eating dinner over at a friend's house. Evan's having a play date, although I don't remember with who."

Laura was lucky enough to have a baby-sitter who chased after her children while she ran around to charity functions. Nina's sister had so many *things*—a baby-sitter, a husband, three kids, two houses, two cars, phones, plants, memberships, and on and on. While Nina, at the moment, felt like she had nothing. Not even an address.

CHAPTER
SEVEN

FORTUNATELY IDA HAD HBO. Sometimes it seemed like the major cultural advantage to an HBO subscription was that you could listen to people say *fuck* on television. But then Rip Torn would come on *The Larry Sanders Show* and everyone would forget about canceling for another couple of days.

Nina was halfway through *Dream On* when the phone rang. She exchanged a look of annoyance with Ida. Fran Lebowitz had once said, in an article entitled "Tips for Teens," that adolescence was the last time you would ever be glad that the phone was for you. Nina found that to be pretty much the case.

"It's your house," she pointed out to her mother.

"Okay, I'll get it." Ida picked up the receiver. "Hello?" she said. "Oh, hi . . . yeah, fine . . . Of course she's here, where else would she be? . . . Okay, I'll get her." Ida handed Nina the phone. "Laura wants to talk to you."

"What's up?" Nina asked her sister.

"Something weird is going on here."

"What's that?"

"After Ken got home from the office, the police came over to question him."

"About what?"

"About Andy's murder, what else?"

"You're kidding. Why Ken?"

"Well, you know that stuff I was telling you about after we got back from Roz's house?"

"Which stuff?" A lot of stuff gets communicated between two women in an afternoon.

"The stuff about the building that Ken and Andy owned together."

"Yeah?"

"Well, it turns out that they owned it as partners with a right of survivorship. Do you know what that means?"

"Joint tenancy with a right of survivorship. Ken gets the building now that Andy's dead. That happens to be one of the few things I do remember from law school." Nina only remembered the human interest side of the law, things like the grounds for divorce. She hadn't a clue as to what the point of a corporation was, nor did she ever get clear the difference between a mortgage and a mortgage note.

Survivorship rights had stuck in her mind. It was easy enough to picture a husband and a wife, or two sisters, buying a piece of property and making sure that when one died the other wouldn't have to share their home with some third party. With a married couple survivorship rights were inherent. With guys like Ken and Andy, it had to be specified.

"Why did they put a right of survivorship into the deal?" she asked Laura. "That's usually for a married couple. It means that Roz is effectively cut out of her inheritance. And that if the tables were turned, you'd be cut out of yours."

"It doesn't matter why they did it. The important thing is that now Ken has become a suspect in Andy's murder."

"Why would a successful Central Park West dermatologist kill someone for half of a rental building in a schlocky neighborhood like Borough Park?" Nina asked.

"He didn't."

"But why would the police even think he did?"

"Well, for one thing, they had just gotten an offer for the building. Ken wanted to sell. But Andy said selling would betray the memory of Mr. Brillstein. That several of his old-time friends, from before the war, were still living there and the only way to be sure that they were treated decently was to hold on to the property."

"So? Partners disagree all the time," Nina said. "That doesn't mean they kill each other. Who do they think Andy and Ken are, Fine and Klein?"

Fine and Klein had meant bargain handbags on the Lower East Side for decades. One day Fine's younger son decided to stage a robbery attempt and have Klein killed so that he could get his hands on all the pocketbooks. Klein escaped, but the business never recovered.

"Besides," Nina continued, "how much can that building be worth?"

"It's not that the building is worth so much. It's just that . . . well, the truth is that it was Ken's idea to go with the survivorship thing. He didn't want to be in the position of owning anything with Roz."

"I can see that she might not be exactly the ideal business partner."

"Even her father knew that. Which is why he put the building in Andy's name to begin with. But nobody wanted to be unfair. So Ken and Andy worked out this deal that the surviving partner would inherit the building with a stipulation that the widow would get a lump-sum payment."

"That seems fair."

"But the amount of the payment increased every year. Because when they bought the building the assumption was that its value would continue to go up. But you know what's happened to real estate in New York City."

"I sure do." It suddenly occurred to Nina that she was having a relatively sophisticated conversation about a legal complexity with her sister, of all people. And Laura was holding her own. Her little JAP-py sister, who sucked her thumb into junior high school and was afraid of the water, now held a driver's license and could discuss an escalation clause without sounding like an idiot.

"When did you get so smart?" Nina asked, sounding more than a little contemptuous. But what else were older sisters for?

"Well, actually, I've gone and gotten my real estate salesperson's license," Laura said. "I thought I might do some part-time work in the neighborhood. In fact, I think I just made my first sale."

"You're kidding."

"No, really. The contract's not signed yet, but the bid's been accepted."

"Why didn't you tell me?"

"I don't know," Laura said.

But Nina knew. Because now Laura was employed and Nina was not. And that was too unbearable to mention. "Congratulations," she forced herself to say.

"Thank you. We'll see how it goes."

"So how serious a suspect do you think Ken is?"

"Well, the police were kind of casual. They didn't talk about arresting him, or tell him not to leave town or anything."

"Have you spoken to Roz about this?"

"Yeah, I called her because I thought that maybe she had started this whole thing. You know, maybe she was pissed when she found out about the survivorship clause and wanted to get even with Ken."

"And?"

"Well, she hadn't known about the building at all before Andy died, and did seem pretty shocked and put out that her husband would hide it from her. But she swears she never suggested to the police that Ken was responsible. She's too busy foaming at the mouth about the fur people."

"The what?"

"The animal rights movement. Roz calls them the fur meshuggeners."

"What do they have to do with anything?"

"She's convinced that they're behind Andy's murder."

"That sounds far-fetched."

"You know," said Laura, "Andy did animal medical research. And the animal rights people were constantly giving him a hard time. Roz always worried about him, working all those weird hours in the lab. She really hated them."

"Well, as the daughter of a furrier she probably had some independent reasons for her hatred."

"Yeah. In a way, that's what brought Roz and Andy together."

"How's that?"

"Well, Andy worked on this herpes vaccine project. He was trying to develop a vaccine by using guinea pigs. So he had to give herpes to all these furry little creatures. Which turned a lot of people off."

Nina tried to remember whether Andy had been droning on about guinea pigs years ago when they had shared a meal. But she couldn't remember any discussion of sexually transmitted diseases in small mammals. She couldn't remember much, just the broiled salmon and a side order of shoestring potatoes.

"So Andy always found himself in the position of having to justify his work," Laura said.

"But not with Roz."

"No, not with Roz. She could give two shits about a bunch of guinea pigs."

"Skin 'em and stitch 'em up, huh?" said Nina. "Just another scrap to trim a hat with."

"That's right."

"No offense to Esmeralda," Nina added. Esmeralda was a Peruvian guinea pig that served as Laura's family's official dog substitute.

"That's okay, Nina. I know that you're fond of Esmeralda in your own way."

Nina liked all kinds of mammals, but had never gotten too worked up over their rights. Most of the real antivivisectionists, she suspected, harbored a true hatred for people rather than a love of animals.

"So what do you think we should do?" asked Laura.

"Do? About what?"

"About Ken. I don't want my husband walking around as a murder suspect."

"Well, I don't know what to tell you."

"Can't you do something? Nina, you're good at this sort of thing."

Nina *was* experienced, if not particularly good at this sort of thing. Even if she wasn't blessed with any particular dexterity for untangling knots, she was the kind of person to whom knots often presented themselves. "Gee," she said, "I'm sure I haven't the faintest—"

"Besides," Laura interrupted, "it'll give you a project. Keep you busy, off the streets."

Now, that hurt. Nina had always been the one who had to squeeze things in, who didn't have a minute. How had she gone from being totally overextended to needing a project to keep her busy?

"Let me think about it," she said. "I'll call you tomorrow."

"What was that all about?" Ida asked after Nina had hung up.

"You got the idea, didn't you?" Nina knew from decades of experience that Ida was highly skilled at extrapolating the unheard half of a telephone conversation.

"Well, sort of," Ida said humbly.

"What do you think I should do? I don't really know where to start."

"Let's talk to Roz first. Don't you think that's a good place for us to start?" Ida asked.

"For us?" When had this turned into a joint project?

"Uh-huh. I could go out there with you."

"Would you really? You know, I'd love it if you'd come with me."

Yeah, so she'd hitchhiked around Europe alone at eighteen. And been elected Camper of the Year two summers in a row. And was known by every baby-sitter in the East Bronx as a kid that never cried when her parents left. She'd proven her independence. But sometimes a girl just needed her mommy.

CHAPTER EIGHT

SURVIVAL INSTINCTS 81

Roz was busy the next day, too busy to meet with Nina and Ida. But the day after that, she had to be in Manhattan anyway, to see her shrink. She agreed to have lunch with them in the Village, after her session. They arranged to meet at a Dean and Deluca's on University Place.

It wasn't the kind of place you went to if you were hungry. No matter what she ever ordered at Dean and Deluca's, Nina always ended up with a plateful of mesclun and a crust of bread. So this morning she made sure to eat a couple of breakfasts before lunch.

Ida's house had slim pickings when it came to noshing. How many bowls of Special K and skim milk could you eat in one sitting? Nina had to resort to prying a bagel out of the freezer and schmearing it with peanut butter that had probably been purchased before Ida had become a grandmother. For a third breakfast, Nina put to rest the remnants of a carton of lowfat frozen something or other, with a raisin-toast chaser.

That was the other bad thing about not working. Besides the lack of salary, you also had to contend with the impulse to eat three breakfasts. The office might be boring or stressful, but at least it promoted a decent interval between meals.

"Enough already," Ida said as she watched the raisin toast disappear. "I thought we were going out to lunch."

"It's healthier to eat early in the day."

Ida didn't dignify that with an answer. "We should go soon," she said.

"I guess. But," Nina added, "I guarantee that Roz is the kind of person who's going to be late."

"But she's coming straight from her therapist."

"She's the kind of person who would have a shrink who was late. And if she did get out of her shrink's on time, she'd stop at a button store or something to make herself late."

"Okay, but let's leave soon anyway," Ida urged.

Roz was late. Even later than Nina expected her to be. But since she was doing them a favor, there didn't seem to be any point to leaving in a huff. Nina and Ida sat at one of the tiny marble tables and watched the staff, which were not only white kids but rich trendy white kids. They moved painfully slowly. If they had been working in a Chinese restaurant, they would have been fired after ten minutes. Why would anyone actually go out of their way to hire white kids to staff a restaurant, much less ones with trust funds? At the pace they were proceeding, you'd think each piece of biscotti weighed twenty pounds.

Roz finally arrived, looking slightly disoriented. She hesitated near the door and Nina got up to meet her. "I'm so sorry," Roz said. "I don't know how the time got away from me. I had to make just one stop on my way over from my shrink, and before I knew it, it was one-thirty." Even though Roz sounded genuine, she still managed to sound like the goddamn queen of England while she apologized.

"That's okay," Nina said. What else was she going to say, anyway?

"But now we'll have to rush. Because I promised Shoshi that I'd go with her to gymnastics today. They're having some little exhibition."

"All right," Nina said. What else was she going to say, anyway? A pattern was emerging. She led Roz over to the table. "This is my mother, Ida Fischman. Roz Brillstein."

"Hello." Ida nodded in a friendly way.

"I'm thrilled to meet you," Roz said. Ida and Nina exchanged a glance of being mutually taken aback. "Laura talks about you all the time," Roz continued. She turned to Nina. "You're so lucky to have her as a mother."

Nina supposed it was true. When she was younger, she had wanted one of those long-legged, golf-playing mothers. But a mother like that would probably have spent years staring at Nina with puzzled despair. And who needed that? Nina had enough puzzled despair to fill her personal quota. Maternal additions were not necessary.

"Is it really true that you're still in therapy?" Roz asked.

"Well, yes." Ida gave a small shrug.

"Well, I think that's absolutely marvelous." Roz made it sound like Ida had just done something thrilling, like finding the cure for AIDS or negotiating peace in the Mideast. Since when had kvetching about the same issues for thirty years without interruption qualified you for the Nobel peace prize?

"What's so marvelous?" Ida said. "I wouldn't wish the same on you."

"Well, the way things are going," Roz said, "I wouldn't be surprised if I beat your record."

Ida put a hand on Roz's shoulder. "I was so sorry to hear about your husband," she said. "I never met him, but Laura and Ken always said that he was a truly lovely man."

"He was." Roz crossed a leg. She was wearing the same black suede boots as last time, but this time they were accompanied by a prewar Persian lamb jacket with a matching hat. It wasn't a look that too many people could pull off, but it looked great on Roz. She slipped out of her jacket, but left her hat perched on her thick red wedge of hair.

"He was a lovely man," Roz continued. "And now he's gone. Just like that." She looked around for a waiter.

"It's self-service," Nina explained.

"Oh." Roz seemed to still be looking for a waiter.

"Can we get you something?" Ida asked.

"Oh, thank you." The idea of a septuagenarian waiting on her was apparently appealing. "What are you having?" Roz asked.

"I don't know. I thought I'd have a grilled vegetable sandwich. On focaccia." You could tell that saying the word *focaccia* gave Ida a thrill, as if she was attending an important cultural event that it was hard to get tickets for.

"That sounds good. I'll have one too," Roz said.

Nina smirked. Women seemed to have a shatterless faith in vegetables, even one that had absorbed four times their weight in olive oil.

"Anything to drink?" Nina asked.

Roz craned her neck to be able to see the beverage display. "I'll have an Orangina."

Nina felt strongly that women's beverage selections spoke volumes. More than their hair, their shoes, their nails, and their earrings, what they drank revealed who they were. The bulk of the gender were water drinkers, shunning excess costs and calories. And their demands for water were always preceded by the word *just* and a little hand flutter. Nina raged internally against the self-abnegation of the "just water" women, although she often found herself a member of their ranks.

You could often predict a woman's preference by her nails. The kind of person who would pay for a professional manicure would often spring for a bottled beverage. The ones with red nails ordered diet Coke, the ones with pale French tips went for designer water. Then there were the real nervous, jumpy nail-biters who ordered black coffee, no matter what time of the day. And bring it right away, please.

More fun and less frantic than the caffeine addicts were the boozers, who had learned enough to enjoy a glass of wine at lunch. Nina liked them best. Second best were the ones willing to imbibe sugar—women who ordered their Cokes without Nutrasweet. But these were rare indeed. Much more common these days were the health food fanatics—freshly squeezed carrot or grapefruit juice, iced cranberry cove tea, or worst of all, just a glass of hot water with a slice of lemon.

But a woman who ordered Orangina was in a class by herself. Basically, Orangina was Fanta with a little less sugar and a little pulp thrown in. Drinking the stuff was hardly any different from guzzling soda pop, a fact that no one acknowledged. For those inclined toward form over substance, Orangina was irresistible. People were willing to drink it because the bottle had an unusual and seductive shape, the label was a compelling shade of blue, and the name was vaguely Italian. The kind of people who collected Bakelite forks.

"An Orangina it is," Nina said, and set off to carry out her mission.

When they were all settled in with their grilled vegetable sandwiches (Ida and Roz) and turkey chili (Nina) and their beverages (which turned out to be Oranginas all around, since Nina and Ida had as strong a tchotchke orientation as the next person), Roz leaned over toward the Fischman women. "What do I owe you?" she asked, without sounding very convincing.

"Oh, please, this is our treat," Ida said. "Thank you so much for taking the time to join us."

"Yes, well, I wasn't certain what you wanted to talk

about." Roz was starting to look and sound guarded. "Was it something about that building in Borough Park? Because I think the terms of the agreement were pretty clear." She was going from guarded to peevish.

"Oh, no. Not at all." Nina stirred her turkey chili while she figured out where to start. "Well, I guess it has something to do with the building. But indirectly. Because if it wasn't for the building, there wouldn't be any reason for the police to suspect Ken of any involvement in Andy's . . . um . . . death." She had stopped herself from using the *M* word at the last minute, since it wasn't clear that Roz had officially come out about the fact that her husband was murdered.

"Please," Roz said. "They can't seriously think that Ken murdered Andy. That's ridiculous and they know it."

"So why would they bother to question him?"

"Just to cover their asses. So that it looks as though they did a thorough investigation. But everyone knows who's really responsible." Roz's eyes narrowed and her mouth stretched into a mean little slit.

"Who's responsible?"

"Those goddamn fur people. Everyone knows that they're crazy and violent. But the Brooklyn D.A.'s office won't touch them."

"Why not?"

"Because the D.A.'s wife is one of them. She's on the board of SPASM."

"SPASM?"

"Society for the Protection of All Small Mammals." Roz stroked the curly black lamb of her hat, but Nina couldn't tell whether the action was subconscious or provocative.

"The D.A.'s wife is active in that organization?"

"Can you believe that a woman married to a law enforcement official hangs out with a bunch of people who break the law on a consistent basis?" Roz hissed. "It seems outrageous, doesn't it? Yet no one does anything to stop it."

"But SPASM's not the group that goes around harassing people, is it?" Ida asked. "Isn't that called something else?"

"You're thinking of AFTA. Association for the Fair Treatment of Animals. But SPASM's just a front for AFTA. It's all the same membership, believe me."

"Why do you think they had something to do with your husband's death?" Ida asked.

"Oh, please. They've been after him for years. I used to worry so much because he always had to work those ridiculous hours. You know, around-the-clock lab experiments that meant he had to be there at three o'clock in the morning. And after driving into Manhattan in the middle of the night, he'd arrive to find that someone had spray-painted his lab with scary, horrible slogans."

Nina couldn't picture it. It sounded to her like Roz was doing a little embroidering. She knew the syndrome, having indulged in it herself. "But how would someone like that have access to Andy's lab?" she asked.

"These people are terrorists. You might think of animal rights activists as harmless little old ladies in sneakers, but that's not true anymore. They know what they're doing and they're vicious. In fact, the guy who's the head of SPASM is a professional agitator, a hired gun. Before he worked for SPASM, he was the public relations director of ACT-UP."

"It's a whole new industry, huh?" Maybe Nina should give him a call. But why bother? When it came to civil unrest, her résumé was hopelessly outdated. She couldn't even remember the last petition she had signed.

"Well, I think it's outrageous," Roz said.

"Have you thought of contacting the press?" Ida asked.

"I mean, if it's really true that the D.A. won't investigate your husband's murder, it sounds like something a reporter would be interested in."

Roz breathed in and out several times, in a deliberate manner, as if practicing a method that she had learned from a trade paperback or on a trip to northern California. She leaned forward and lowered her voice. "I'm concerned about spreading this around. I'd rather not use the word *murder* to too many people."

"I don't understand," Nina said. But then she did. No matter how much of a happy melting pot America was in the fifties, no matter how booming the economy, no matter how brightly the Statue of Liberty's torch had shone at the time, being born in a displaced person's camp was not something that just faded away, like a strawberry birthmark on the back of an infant's neck.

CHAPTER NINE

IDA AND NINA WATCHED Roz's perky little hat bob down University Place. "What did you think?" Nina asked. "Fruitcake? Or just your run-of-the-mill New York neurotic?"

"She's a complicated woman."

"Don't give me that noncommittal bullshit," she told her mother. "Who are you, the goddamn president of General Motors? Answer the question."

"Um, fruitcake, I guess."

"Yeah, I think so too."

"Speaking of fruitcake," Ida said, "would you be interested in splitting a pear tartlet?"

"I see you've already perused the dessert menu."

"Well, the pear tartlets did catch my eye."

"Don't you think that something called a tartlet would be too small to split?" Nina asked.

"Not necessarily."

"I once split a crème brûlée with someone. My half-portion was so tiny, I wept. I'd rather go without than be stuck with something so heartbreakingly undersized."

"Oh, forget it," Ida said. "I'll stop on the street for a Tastee Delight."

"What's that? One of those eight-calorie-an-ounce things that taste like Kaopectate?"

"Exactly."

"You shouldn't eat fake food, you know. It can't be good for you."

They took a meandering route home, making stops at the Greenmarket in Union Square for homemade pretzels and at Eileen Fisher to see what was on sale. Not that Nina needed new clothes. She had a working wardrobe and she didn't even work. But she couldn't get enough of the drably colored, shapeless garments they sold at the loftlike shop on lower Fifth Avenue.

Today she toyed with a pair of wide-legged rayon trousers that came in three shades. One was the color of a subway token that had passed from hand to hand for twenty years without being taken out of circulation. The second reminded Nina of the walls of the elementary school that she had attended. The other was something like the color of the water in a bucket after a mop had been rinsed out.

Nina thought back to all the brightly colored, tightly fitting garments she had worn over the years—her purple leotard, her red patent leather belt, a short satin bolero that was canary-yellow on the outside and lime-green on the inside. And the beads and the feathers and the suede fringe—all gone. Replaced by an oversize drape of muddy rayon. What was she in mourning for?

Ida didn't get it. She still wore purple and roped plenty of beads around her neck. "Elegance is refusal," some skinny rich broad had once said. Ida refused to refuse. As a result, she certainly didn't look elegant. But even if she was no duchess of Windsor, she looked a whole lot happier than her daughter. Nina decided to pass on the pants. They hadn't been marked down yet and in her current unemployed state, she'd have plenty of time to check for subsequent sales.

• • •

Ida's answering machine was blinking when they got home, and it was Jonathan's voice that sprang forth from the tape. "Nina, please call me. I'm coming back East for Thanksgiving and I'd like to see you. I miss you." He sounded so nice. Their last days had been so fraught with anger and disappointment and guilt, she had forgotten that Jonathan was basically a normal person.

Ida had the grace to say nothing and let Nina go outside for a walk without comment. The walk turned into a movie, something cute and stupid with Hugh Grant. Nina had always favored male movie stars who weren't too heavy on the testosterone, who could have been her college roommate's bisexual boyfriend.

By the time she got back to her mother's, it was dark and she was ready to make the call. He'd still be in the office, with the time difference and all, and she could just picture his secretary's eyebrows shooting up when she realized it was Nina calling. But she didn't want to be sitting around, huddled in her bathrobe at midnight with her breasts flopping, waiting to call him at home. Nina decided to capitalize on the momentum of a brisk walk up Broadway and picked up the phone without breaking her stride.

He answered his own phone. "It's Nina," she said, trying not to sound as if she was admitting some weakness.

"Nina, I'm so glad to hear from you. How are you?"

He seemed to expect an answer. She felt her pulse to make sure she was still alive and tried to figure out what to say. There was no point in pretending that everything was great, because she was never good at pulling that off, even when she wasn't unemployed and living with her mother. On the other hand, many people made the mistake of thinking that the person on the other end of the line really wanted to know the ins and outs, the ups and downs, all the contours of your troubles. And that was

never the case, unless the person was a really morbid suc-
cubus, who got physical sustenance from other people's
tsouris. And why would you give a person like that your
phone number in the first place?

So Nina played the middle ground, telling Jonathan a
charming little story about how everyone in the audience
during weekday afternoon movies seemed to be pushing
eighty and you could hardly hear the dialogue because
everyone was coughing and commenting and yelling
"What did she say?" every minute.

Jonathan laughed and said that he missed New York
because of things like that. But he said it in a way that
people who are never coming back say it. With that hint
of haughtiness which lets you know that they feel like
they escaped by the skin of their teeth.

"The reason I called," he said, obviously not thinking
that Nina's mere existence constituted enough of a reason, "is that I'm coming in next week on business. And if
you're available, I thought you might come to my parents'
house for Thanksgiving dinner."

What did this mean? What significance did this re-
quest have? Perhaps he meant that he wanted to get back
together with her. That he'd quit his job, was moving
back East to be with Nina, and planned on presenting her
with an engagement ring between the roast turkey and
the pumpkin pie. That was the least likely scenario. It was
infinitely more probable, now that they were no longer
living together, now that he was no longer invested in
their relationship, that he suddenly was able to bring her
home to meet his mother. Now that it didn't matter. Or
maybe he was just a nice guy and thought Nina might be
interested in a free dinner and in being just friends.

"Just friends" meant different things to different people. In the movies, whenever there was a blond waitress in
a truck stop who kept getting knocked up by guitar-play-

ing rats who looked like Sam Shepard, a man who wanted to be just friends was a godsend. But to women like Nina, who weren't exactly the truck-stop type, the words had the painful emotional connotations of a junior high school dance.

Maybe Jonathan wasn't thinking of anything, not engagement rings or just friends, but felt like seeing Nina and thought she might brighten up a dreary family dinner. Who cares what he's thinking, she told herself. Get beyond that gender affliction of figuring out what the other person really wants and why he wants it. Decide what *you* want.

Of course Nina knew that it didn't really matter what she wanted, since she was bound to accept his invitation. She had long been the kind of person who said yes to almost every offer. Which had been a problem when she was younger and still hitchhiked. But she never wanted to miss any opportunities, having had the kind of childhood where nothing ever happened. And lately it seemed that her life was turning back to those days in the Bronx— frozen bagels and late-night television and her mother in the next room.

So of course she'd go to Thanksgiving dinner. Besides, even though she had always dreaded meeting Jonathan's mother (whom he had described as a cross between Rose Kennedy and Don Rickles), Nina was dying of curiosity.

"Oh," she said. "Um . . . gee. I guess maybe. That is, I was going to go out to my sister's beach house, and you know how much I love it there."

"Well, I don't know if an evening with my mother is going to be any better."

"I know, I know, Rose Kennedy, right?"

"Well, don't say I didn't warn you."

"If she's half as . . . um . . . dynamic as you've described, it'll be worth it."

"Yeah, I'm sure you won't be disappointed."

"So how long are you staying?" she asked.

"I couldn't get a flight back on Sunday, so I'm leaving on Saturday." She wasn't imagining it; he definitely sounded apologetic. How could he forget so soon that it was she who had left him? If anyone should feel guilty, it was Nina. And if anyone should feel hurt, it was Jonathan. How had the tables turned so quickly?

"I'll come pick you up on Thursday," he said. "Around two, is that okay?"

"Sure."

"You'll be at your mother's?"

"Yeah." She felt like a charity case. This whole thing was a mistake; she should definitely cancel. But that chance to catch a glimpse of Mrs. Harris after all this time still proved irresistible.

CHAPTER
TEN

IDA HAD CLEARLY HEARD every word. And since she was in a position of strength, she could afford to sit back and let her daughter initiate the conversation.

Nina held back for a couple of minutes, but after a while her silence began to feel like posturing. "So do you think I'm making a mistake?" she asked her mother.

"Who's to say?"

"I'm asking you because I value your opinion." Nina choked up a little at the end of the sentence. In Jewish families, people generally avoided saying anything nice to each other. It was some sort of incest taboo.

"Nina, this isn't *Jeopardy*. There are no right and wrong answers."

"What would you have done?"

"Me? I'm no paragon of sensibility. I'm just like you, dying of curiosity to get a look at his mother. In fact, I might just come along. The hell with my grandchildren. They can get through Thanksgiving without me."

Nina knew she was kidding. And she appreciated Ida's support. But sometimes she wished she had a mother who was a little better schooled in the rules of comportment, who wasn't such an anarchist at heart. Who had told her to be sure to be married by thirty and to wait until her first child was out of diapers before she got pregnant again. Instead of just stumbling through life, hoping she'd bump up against some interesting tangent to go off on.

"If you're worried that you made some fatal mistake," Ida said, "don't be. I mean, it doesn't seem to me that you particularly want Jonathan back. It was *you* who left *him*, after all."

"So why doesn't it feel that way?"

"Nothing ever feels that way. Listen, go to dinner, cross-examine the woman, and report back. You have nothing to lose."

"Yeah, you're right. Nothing to lose." *Freedom's just another word for nothing left to lose.* Well, in that case, Nina had never been freer.

"There's no point in obsessing about Thanksgiving," Ida said.

"What else am I supposed to obsess about?"

"What should we do about Roz?" Ida sounded like she was suggesting a rainy-day project to a cranky child.

"I don't know, what should we do about Roz?" Nina said, whining like a cranky child.

"Well, all that stuff about the animal rights people sounded pretty interesting, didn't it?"

"I don't know. You buy all that about the D.A.'s wife? Sounded like a crock to me."

"Considering Roz's evident talent for histrionics," Ida said, "it could well be a crock. But I've found that when you look closely, most things are not a total crock. There's no such thing as spontaneous generation, even when it comes to rumors."

"I suppose. But how are we supposed to investigate the animal rights movement? I wouldn't know where to begin."

"Don't you know anyone who's active? You're an animal lover, aren't you?" Ida asked.

"Just because I wanted a puppy when I was six years

old doesn't make me an animal lover, for chrissakes." Ida, being only one generation away from the shtetl, still conformed to the notion that pets were for goyim.

"Well, pretend you're a reporter. That seems to work when they do it on television."

"That's silly."

"Or better yet," Ida said, slipping back into her rainy-day project voice, "why don't you actually get yourself an assignment? You always were a good writer."

"A good writer and an animal lover. That's me. And how am I supposed to get such an assignment?"

"Call your friend Ellen Simon."

"Ma, Ellen's not my friend. She never was. She's just someone I sort of know." Ellen Simon was the kind of girl —there was one in every high school—who everyone's parents loved. They all hocked their daughters to befriend her. She was editor of the Bronx Science newspaper, she didn't smoke dope, and she wore her hair back, out of her face. Destined for success. Nina always thought she was a suck-up and a phony, but not without some charisma. Ellen was smart, that was for sure, and she knew how to play an angle. Nina and Ellen became friends once removed, and they maintained their semifriendship throughout the years. Ellen Simon graduated from the Columbia School of Journalism (the "J" School, as it was called) and gained some fame as an Anna Quindlen–type columnist for *New York Newsday*, writing about her perfect family. When she discarded her first husband for a richer one, she also had to discard the column and dodge the hate mail. So she switched to a more investigative format, but still threw in occasional details about her former mother-in-law. Now that *Newsday* had receded back to the shores of Long Island, Ellen had managed to syndicate her column.

She and Nina had lunch about twice a decade and

Ellen would always make such a fuss about how the world still needed "do-gooders" like Nina. But you could tell that she'd rather be dead than live Nina's life for even a day. Ellen Simon was the kind of woman who would fight like a tigress over a manicure appointment.

"I don't think my ego's up for a phone call to Ellen Simon."

"Look." Ida actually pointed her finger at Nina. "You have some very interesting information. There's an allegation that the Brooklyn district attorney is suppressing a murder investigation because of his wife's involvement in . . . what's the name of the group again? ORGASM?"

"SPASM. Society for the Protection of All Small Mammals."

"Right. Ellen Simon's specialty is uncovering local scandals. You're holding all the cards here. She should take you to lunch and pick up the check."

"Yeah, right. If I'm lucky she'll return the phone call."

"Why don't you at least try?" Ida said.

"Nah, I'd rather sit around watching *Letterman* and eating raisin toast."

"Come on, just call. Nothing to lose."

"Nothing left to lose. What the hell." Nina dialed Ellen Simon at home. Some housekeeper-type person answered the phone and said that Ellen would be home around eight. She had to spell Fischman a couple of times, but the woman finally got it. And much to Nina's amazement, Ellen Simon called her back before eight-thirty.

"Nina, this is Ellen. Did you call me?" In addition to still wearing her hair back, Ellen had eyes that bugged out a bit. And her voice had the same hyperthyroidy quality.

"Yeah, Ellen, thanks for returning the call. How are you?"

"On overload as usual. But okay. How are you?"

Nina knew enough not to mention how she had suddenly found herself on underload. Underload would not play well with Ellen Simon. "I'm fine. Just back from L.A. I was out there for a couple of months."

"My condolences." If Ellen Simon chose to live on the East Coast, then that was the only coast to live on.

"Yeah, that's pretty much how I felt. Which is why I came back. Anyway, a strange thing happened last week, which I thought might make an interesting column."

"What's that?" Ellen's voice was guarded, as if every time she walked down the street, some passerby would pick up a piece of dreck out of the gutter and tell her he thought it would make a good column.

"A friend of my brother-in-law's died suddenly. He lived in Brooklyn and worked at Morgan University, doing medical research on animals. Apparently he was poisoned and his wife claims that it was the animal rights people who did it."

"Has anyone been charged?"

"Well, that's the thing. The wife says that the Brooklyn D.A. won't touch it because his wife is on the board of SPASM, one of the organizations she thinks was involved."

"I've heard of them." You really didn't exist if Ellen Simon hadn't heard of you.

"I thought that maybe I could do some research about this. And if it turned into anything, you could break the story."

"Well, ordinarily I'd say that the whole thing sounds like total conjecture. You haven't given me any evidence to back up anything she said. But I'll let you in on a little secret of mine."

"What's that?" Nina forced herself to project the proper mix of excitement and gratitude.

"I absolutely hate the Brooklyn D.A. Ed Daley is the most pompous, condescending, loathsome human being I have ever had the misfortune to meet."

"I'm sure he is." Takes one to know one.

"And if there's any way I can loosen his corrupt grip on Kings County, I'd be delighted."

"Well, I thought that if I could say that I was working for you, it would give me some legitimacy and get me through some doors that would ordinarily shut in my face."

"Of course it would. Although I have to admit that after all these years, there are plenty of people who would slam their door just because you mentioned Ellen Simon."

Nina believed it. "If you'd like," she said, "I can just say I'm doing research on an article without using your name."

"You know what? I've just been commissioned to do a freelance piece for *The New Yorker*. A local political roundup. They gave me about two months to finish it. Maybe we can work this into it. Why don't you just tell people that you're researching an article for *The New Yorker*. That way I can pay you out of my research budget."

So not only had *The New Yorker* hired Ellen Simon to write for them, they had given her a research budget. The most manipulative and self-promoting girl at Bronx Science was writing for *The New Yorker*. William Shawn would have thrown Ellen out of his office in thirty seconds. But Nina could see how Tina Brown might think she was a real find.

"Just be sure to give me a weekly report," Ellen said. "Call in on Friday. If I'm not at my desk, just leave it on my voice mail. And I'll check and see how much money I can get for you."

"Sounds good." Well, that wasn't bad. With just one phone call, Nina had gone from being unemployed to working for *The New Yorker*.

CHAPTER
ELEVEN

WITH THE FORCE of *The New Yorker* behind her, Nina decided to start at the top. The executive director of
SPASM was Peter Slater and he had been anxious to meet
with Nina when she called. All she had to do was tell him
when and where, and he even showed up without being
late. Not only that, but he was gorgeous. Perhaps she had
finally entered a world where men were gorgeous and not
late. It was as if after forty years of living in the city, she
had magically passed from one side of a line to another,
over to the side where she got to call all the shots. Or at
least this one shot.

He had the kind of coloring that no one in New York
ever has. The kind you find only in Minneapolis and Swe-
den. A blond who tans, with hair, eyes, and skin that just
melt together into a golden glow. His nostrils were flared
in an attractive, horsey way and his lips were as full as last
year's fashion models'. His hair was thick and cut short in
a retro, crew-cut kind of thing. But instead of being spiky
it had the soft, velvety look of a deep-pile broadloom.

Nina had to sit on her hands. She wanted to pat his
hair, trace his lips, stick her finger in his nose. What
would it be like, she wondered, to be the kind of person
who people couldn't keep their hands off of? Roz had said
something about Slater being formerly associated with
ACT-UP, the militant AIDS group. Was he gay?

Gay was probably an oversimplification. Men and women were probably the tip of the iceberg as far as Peter Slater's sexuality went. Dogs undoubtedly ran after him in the street, desperate for a chance to lick his hand. Nina was sure that babies reached up to him from their strollers, that horses craned their necks to nuzzle the fine nostrils that so resembled their own. How does a person like that make choices? When every bit of protoplasmic flotsam and jetsam is throwing itself at you, how do you decide what to fend off? It was like being rich and thin—how do you ever stop shopping?

Calm down, Nina told herself. Peter Slater is not the sexual messiah, simply a good-looking guy. Just because you want to poke his face and pat his hair doesn't mean that everybody else in the world does.

"Nice to meet you." He extended a hand that tapered into long, artistic fingers. Jesus, even this guy's knuckles looked good. And he had the voice of a man who did public speaking for a living. A pleasant, nonlocalized accent with enough bass tones to let you know that there was a healthy amount of testosterone flowing. Not the kind of voice that you wanted to turn down the volume on, the kind you heard on the subway or in the office whining about the price of a new car or this year's tax bill. But the kind that made you insatiable for more. Peter Slater's voice was a powerful, manipulative tool.

She wondered how old he was. It was hard to tell, somewhere between twenty-five and forty-five. Only one thing was absolutely certain—he was in his prime.

They were in his office, the national headquarters of SPASM. Nina had expected a ratty place, filled with used cardboard coffee cups and folding chairs. Instead, the place was very respectable, with an address on a good block near Grand Central Station, unworn carpeting, unstained upholstery, and a receptionist who had good teeth.

"Pretty spiffy quarters," she said, as she allowed herself to make hand contact with Peter Slater. She had to avert her eyes from his, however, since simultaneous hand and eye contact might prevent her from remaining erect.

"What did you expect?" he asked, releasing her hand all too quickly for her taste.

"Someplace grimier. More volunteerish and temporary. Less professional."

"SPASM has been in existence for almost thirty years. We're a reputable organization. The members of our board of directors are an illustrious bunch. Several also sit on the boards of the philharmonic, the Metropolitan Museum of Art, and the Ford Foundation. We're not some crackpot fringe group, not by any means."

"Not like AFTA?"

"AFTA serves an important function in the animal rights movement. As an activist organization they are able to bring public attention to various issues, while we do more of the behind-the-scenes work."

"Some people say that SPASM is nothing more than a front for AFTA."

"Not true, not true at all." He didn't raise his voice. He didn't even sound particularly emphatic. He sounded like one of those four-hundred-dollar-per-hour lawyers who sound truthful and convincing, though you never know whether to believe them or not. "We're discrete organizations. Although our membership lists do overlap."

His casual but correct use of *discrete* started Nina thinking. This guy was gorgeous and articulate and on time. He should have his own talk show, or at least a minor cult following. How much money could he be making sitting behind this desk? She inspected him for evidence of personal wealth.

It was often hard to tell with men. If they were wearing a well-cut denim shirt with khakis, as Slater was, they could be rich and straight or poor and gay. Or they might have gone to Dartmouth on a scholarship or just have a girlfriend with classy taste. Supposedly you could tell by the watch. But Nina, who had come of age in a time when no one wore watches (or carried umbrellas), was not good at judging watches. Slater wore a thin gold one, with a nondescript brown leather band. Was thin good in a watch, the way it was in a woman? Did "less is more" hold true for timepieces? She just didn't know.

She looked at his feet. He was wearing rugged oxfords made from a drab matte green leather. Each shoe sported a small label that said "Mephisto." Nina had heard of this brand of shoe. It was supposed to be very comfortable and very expensive. Not expensive in a Ferragamo kind of way, but expensive in a three-figure sneaker kind of way. But that didn't mean he was rich, she supposed, since kids all over Harlem were wearing three-figure sneakers.

Mephisto. Was Peter Slater evil? He was so desirable, it was hard not to connect him with a sense of danger. And his pansexual quality, which she was so sure would appeal to all animate objects, crossed so many boundaries that it had to give off a mix of thrills and chills. Nina herself was both thrilled and chilled to be in his presence.

But that was not why she was here. So she took one last look at his sneakers and his watch and then plunged ahead.

"Mr. Slater, I am going to be perfectly honest about why I'm here. There have been allegations about the cover-up of a murder. And your organization has been mentioned as having some potential involvement."

"A murder? SPASM? That's ridiculous." He said it in the same nonemphatic, four-hundred-dollar-per-hour way. "Who was murdered?"

"A man named Andrew Campbell. He was a medical researcher at Morgan University who was testing a herpes vaccine on guinea pigs. According to his wife, he received constant threats while he was alive."

"Threats from SPASM members?"

"It's unclear who the threats were from. But someone in the animal rights movement had it in for him. And Campbell's widow doesn't think that the Brooklyn D.A. is adequately investigating your group because his wife is on your board."

"Oh, yes. Dottie Daley." Peter Slater gave Nina an enigmatic smile, which gave off bits of both contempt and warmth. It was hard to figure out what he thought of Dottie Daley.

"So is she on the board?"

"Of course. Dottie is one of our more active members. Have you ever met her?"

"No."

"You should. You're not likely to ever meet anyone else like her."

"In what way?"

"In every way. You'd have to meet her to even begin to see what I mean."

"Would she do something like that? Tell her husband not to investigate?"

"Dottie?" He grinned again. "Yeah, she would. But he wouldn't listen."

"What do you mean?"

"Dottie would tell anybody anything. She says whatever she thinks. And she says it loudly. She used to be a big antiabortion activist, but she switched to animals a couple of years ago."

"How come?"

"Frankly, I think her husband asked her to. The abortion stuff was too much of a political hot potato for Ed.

So now she bills herself as a pro-lifer who's concentrating on small mammals. Innocent life includes minks, that sort of thing."

"I see," Nina said. "Could I meet her? Do you think she would talk to me?"

"Sure. She'll talk to anybody. She loves to talk. I don't think that she reads *The New Yorker,* but she'll meet with you. Tell her I gave you her number." Slater ripped a piece of paper from a pad and scribbled a phone number on it.

Nina noticed that he didn't have to check his Rolodex for the number. It made her wonder about the nature of the relationship between Dottie Daley and Peter Slater. "Um, how old is she?" Nina asked.

"Dottie?" He broke out in yet another enigmatic grin. "Dottie is forever young."

"Oh, okay. Well, why don't you tell me something about SPASM." Nina pulled a steno pad out of her purse and fished around for a pen.

"Here you go." Slater handed her a ballpoint.

"Thanks."

"My pleasure," he said. A guy who looked as good as Peter Slater couldn't really use the word *pleasure* without giving his audience all sorts of ideas. So as he launched into his monologue describing the guiding principles and historical context of SPASM, Nina's mind wandered to places where it didn't belong at the moment. And by the end of the interview, instead of finding herself with pages full of crisp, concise notes, she discovered that she had filled her pad with doodles that had an embarrassingly obvious phallic content to them.

CHAPTER
TWELVE

PETER SLATER WAS RIGHT. Dottie Daley would be thrilled to talk to her. "Oh, yes. *The New Yawker*," she said, remembering to put the *r* at the end of the word, but forgetting to put it in the middle. "I read it every week. It's my favorite magazine."

Dottie gave Nina very explicit directions to her house out on Cortelyou Road. But Nina was nervous the whole way anyway, as she always was when she took the subway to Brooklyn. She would occasionally still have that old nightmare, left over from her Bronx childhood, and dream that she was on the BMT, the old kind with the wicker seats and revolving ceiling fans, and forget to get off in Manhattan. And there she'd be, barreling through the East River subway tunnel, heading for the uncharted territory of Kings County.

Of course, she had taken the IRT countless times to her sister's house in Park Slope. But brownstone Brooklyn was arguably an extension of Manhattan. Cortelyou Road, on the other hand, was farther out, where people had driveways, and it meant taking the D train. Which wasn't technically the BMT, but it wasn't the IRT either. Basically the Bronx was the Bronx, Brooklyn was Brooklyn, and the twain were natural enemies. The fact that her borough had burned down before their borough never ceased to annoy her, even though she had fled the Bronx decades ago.

The truth was that Nina was no longer a little girl with the BMT wicker seats sticking into her legs and she was quite capable of navigating from West End Avenue to Cortelyou Road. She didn't get lost once, and she actually found herself enjoying the sights of this well-preserved Victorian section of Flatbush. The neighborhood was heavily populated with high-ranking municipal employees, people who wanted to own a house but were required to live in the city because of their jobs. People who probably would have taken off for Montclair or Dobbs Ferry if it had been up to them.

The Daley house stuck out from the rest of the block because of the garish border of still-blooming annuals that trimmed the driveway. The other houses featured quiet, dignified perennials that had long since succumbed to autumnal frosts. But marigolds and zinnias and asters and even a few impatiens made a showy display in front of the house, which itself was painted a slightly too loud shade of yellow.

Dottie Daley's hair was a different kind of yellow, more orangey but just as loud. It matched the marigolds in the driveway. Her hair was cut short, but everything else was generously proportioned. She was tall, broad-shouldered, amply bosomed, long-legged, and full-hipped. Larger than life. She wore orange pants that used to be called pedal pushers with a matching top and size eleven gold mules.

It wasn't exactly mule and pedal pusher weather. Nina was wearing her usual assortment of black and gray wool garments, the assemblage of which portrayed a kind of "Siege of Stalingrad" look. There were plenty of quiet, drab women out there who made Nina feel absolutely florid despite her cossack wardrobe. But Dottie Daley wasn't one of them. Nina knew, just by looking at her, that they would polarize each other. And that Dottie would get louder and more colorful and Nina would suddenly get quieter and smaller and better behaved and start acting like she had grown up in Scarsdale.

"Come on in," Dottie said, grabbing Nina by the wrist instead of shaking her hand. "You didn't have any trouble finding the place, did you?"

"No, you gave me excellent directions. Thank you."

"Because you sounded mighty nervous when I mentioned the D train." Dottie gave a sonic boom of a laugh, making Nina feel more Scarsdale-like than ever. A thought crossed Nina's mind like a cloud. Dottie Daley was probably younger than her. And yet her front hall was filled with photographs of absolutely gigantic children.

Dottie caught her staring at them. "I won't bother telling you their names," she said. "Because you won't be able to keep them straight."

"How many are there?"

"Five."

"And how old are they?"

"The oldest is twenty. I got started early."

"They're so big."

"They're huge. The biggest is six-five. It's my genes. I've got a brother who's six-seven."

"Really? Wow."

"Come into the kitchen. I'll make you some tea." That was one of the best things about being in an Irish household. Someone would make you some really good tea, like in the old country. Jews had never sat around the shtetl making each other tea. Once in a while, however, they would pluck you a chicken.

Nina entered the Daley kitchen, which was filled with corny tchotchkes of every conceivable variety. A lot of them had a Celtic theme; there were many mentions of shamrocks and Guinness and KISS ME I'M IRISH was cross-stitched on a linen sampler. Perhaps her kitchen collection was not museum quality, but Dottie Daley brewed the real thing from loose tea in a ceramic pot that had been prewarmed with a splash of boiling water. And she seemed genuinely warm as she told Nina how she had gotten involved in the animal rights movement.

"I'm not really an animal lover; that's the funny thing about it. For example, you'll notice that there are no pets around here."

"Oh." It was true, there were no bowls of cat food, no animal hairs, no doggie smell lingering in the air.

"But I believe in life. In the life of an unborn fetus and in the life of a rhesus monkey." Dottie Daley was one of those people who managed to sound remarkably articulate despite a heavy New York accent. "But it took me a while to sort things out. My neighbor, Doris Milstein, is a big animal person. The Milsteins have a huge house, but never had any children. She keeps the place filled up with King Charles spaniels and Abyssinian kittens. Quite frankly, it stinks over there. I mean, my kids are slobs, but at least they don't smell."

"Actually," Nina said, "it smells really good in here. Something lemony."

"Yeah, I just finished polishing the dining room table. I'm something of a cleanliness freak."

Nina wondered whether she would ever have the kind of life where she polished things. Her present existence, composed as it was of suede shoes and stainless steel flatware, did not require any polishing at all.

"Anyway, when Doris first asked me to volunteer in her organization, I thought she was crazy. I told her that I had five kids to worry about, why should I spend time on a bunch of animals?"

"Sounds reasonable."

"But then I thought it might set a good example for

Conor. He's my oldest and used to be quite a bully. I figured if I could get him involved in helping weaker creatures, it might spill over into his attitude toward his classmates. So Conor and I went off to some event they were having at the animal shelter and the most amazing thing happened."

"What was that?"

"My husband came with us. Ed never has time to go anywhere, but he made an exception for this. And Conor was so thrilled, because he hardly ever gets to see his father."

"Your husband must be very busy."

"Well, to tell you the truth, Ed hasn't always been thrilled about my political activities. He claims that he's been successful in spite of me, not because of me. I guess he figured that I couldn't get into too much trouble over a bunch of animals. And Conor was so sweet with the pets, a totally different boy than he was in the schoolyard."

"How nice." Nina finished her tea. It was excellent, as predicted.

"So we started spending more time at the shelter and then I joined SPASM and the next thing I knew, I had been elected to their board of directors."

"I see."

"Well, I guess the fact that my husband is the district attorney of Kings County didn't hurt." Dottie said it without pretension.

"Who knows?"

"The funny thing is that when I first met Ed Daley, I thought he was another hopeless cause." She leaned toward Nina for intimacy. "I was dating a Jewish guy named Barry whose father was a dentist. Ed was just one of that swarm of guys from Bishop Ford that hung around my cousin Timothy. I figured I could see Ed twenty years in the future, working for Con Ed and stopping off on his way home every night. Well, he showed me. And he showed everybody else too."

"What happened to Barry?"

"Oh, he's out in Great Neck. On his third wife, from what I hear."

There was a break in the conversation. Dottie looked at her watch. Nina decided it was time for action. "Dottie," she said, "I can tell that you're the kind of person who says what she thinks. So I'm going to repay you in kind and tell you exactly why I'm here."

"Shoot."

"Well, I'm writing this article about SPASM and AFTA. But I'm also investigating the murder of a researcher at Morgan University. His name was Andy Campbell and he did medical experiments on guinea pigs. Apparently, everyone in his lab had received threats from animal rights activists. So when he showed up dead, some people were suspicious."

"Yeah? And?"

"And thought that some of the membership might have been involved."

"That's baloney." The old-fashioned phrase brought back a flood of memories, the way a smell or an old song will. There was a time, which Nina barely remembered, when the Irish still ran New York City. Robert Wagner was mayor and Mrs. Delaney was Nina's fourth-grade teacher and people still said things like "that's baloney" and "you're full of malarkey." And people like Dottie Daley and Ralph Kramden lived all over the boroughs and assumed that their children would never move out of their parish. Dottie was a holdout, who now lived next door to a crazy Jewish cat lady because everyone she grew up with had moved away.

"Will you let me tell you something?"

"Do I have a choice?"

"No."

"I didn't think so."

"I'll admit that some of our members are pretty crazy. They're not really people persons, if you know what I mean. They prefer to relate to animals, so it stands to reason that some of them don't have the best of personalities."

"In other words," Nina said, "these are people that were probably not popular in high school."

"Right. But I know that none of them would kill someone. They're pro-life."

"So how do you explain people who run around shooting the doctors at abortion clinics?"

Dottie shook her head. "That wouldn't happen in New York," she said, as if it were an explanation. "But do you want to know something?"

"What?"

"No matter how crazy some of our members are, I still think that those researchers are crazier."

"Why?"

"What kind of person would want to spend his working day killing small, furry creatures? If you're looking for a murderer, that's the place to look. In the lab. Anyone who could inject a hundred mice with toxic substances could easily kill a human being."

"Andy Campbell died at home in Brooklyn. Has anyone been charged with the murder? Are the police investigating? Is your husband's office involved?"

"I just don't know," Dottie said. "This is the first I've heard of the incident."

Nina shrugged. Dottie Daley was the kind of person you just had to believe. But Nina couldn't tell whether you had to believe her because she always told the truth or because she was such a brilliant liar.

CHAPTER THIRTEEN

JONATHAN'S MOTHER looked nothing like what Nina had expected. All this time, Nina had variously imagined Margaret Thatcher, Nancy Reagan, or Katharine Hepburn without the tremor. Mrs. Harris looked like none of these women. Basically, Mrs. Harris looked like an old Jewish lady.

She wasn't dressed like one, of course. She was wearing navy and white, colors that Nina associated with Connecticut and Christianity. And her hair was cut in an unlayered, undyed gray bob. Nina rarely met a Jewish woman who could resist both layering and dyeing simultaneously. Mrs. Harris's nails were short, her heels were low, her voice was soft. But the nose, the legs, the lips, the earlobes, all the uncontrollable features were large and lumpy and . . . well . . . Jewish.

Mrs. Harris had the Simone Signoret syndrome. One day you're in a black slip, kissing Laurence Harvey, and the next thing you know you're in support hose, getting your veins done.

"Call me Marilyn," she had murmured when introduced to Nina. Marlene Dietrich had been wrong. It's not the legs that are the last to go, it's the murmur. Nina wasn't used to Jews who murmured, but she had promised herself this morning that she was going to be open-minded.

She had made that promise before Jonathan arrived to pick her up. His arrival, of course, hadn't clarified a thing. He was warm and affectionate and she was glad to see him, but still glad that she wasn't living in California. When she opened the door, she had expected some dramatic plot point, something that made it all clear. A strong feeling in her gut that she had made the best decision of her life or else a terrible mistake. She found neither on the other side of the threshold, just a five-eleven, slightly chubby question mark wearing khaki pants and a blue oxford shirt.

He brought her a present, a coffee mug with some snotty joke about lawyers on it. Nina tended to forget that she was a lawyer and therefore never took lawyer jokes personally. But Jonathan had always been slightly in awe of her bar admission, in a way that only someone who had attended art school could be.

She had agonized over what to wear that morning, knowing that if the time had ever come to look thin and classy, it was now. But she wanted to look a little bohemian, as well. After all, she was trying to pull off being unemployed. She ultimately decided on forest-green as a color that straddled the subcultures of Greenwich, Connecticut, and Greenwich Village. A color with intelligence and, in the right setting, a modicum of elitism. Which would play well with Jonathan's parents.

The hard decision, as always, was jewelry. A friend had once shared something she had been taught by her mother. Put on your jewelry, she said, and then take off one piece. But it was no help, really, since it always pushed Nina into obsessing about which piece to remove. She did, however, refrain from getting an extra hole pierced in her ears.

Today she played it safe—small garnet earrings, a watch, and an amber ring that she had bought in some foreign bazaar twenty years ago. Nina thought fleetingly that the amber and garnet might not match. But then she remembered that the same friend who told her to take off one piece of jewelry had told her that *match* is a word used only by people who had flocked wallpaper in their bathrooms.

Marilyn Harris wore a few small pieces of marcasite set with pearls. Nina owned neither marcasite nor pearls, never having thought of herself as that kind of person. But she had to admit that it was an appealing combination. Now that she was forty, maybe she was ready for such things. She would have to look into it.

The Harris house was in Douglaston, technically in the borough of Queens, but it could have been anywhere in the Northeast where affluent people grew roses. The smell from the kitchen was promising. Marilyn Harris explained that she had bought some figs for the stuffing, but as it turned out she had too many. So she had put together a fig and blackberry cobbler for dessert.

Norman Harris finally emerged from somewhere, so it was time for drinks. He looked a little like Jonathan, but with extra height. Always dangerous, Nina thought, when the father is taller than the son. Amazing what havoc a mere few inches can wreak in terms of family dynamics. Jonathan had described him as your typical controlling bastard, but the man who stood before Nina looked benign, just some old guy who you wouldn't be afraid to tell to stop talking during a movie.

He fixed himself a Bombay martini, which sounded more interesting than it was. Nina had an image of a cardamom pod floating in place of an olive, but it turned out to be just a plain old martini made with the Bombay brand of gin. Jonathan had a beer and Mrs. Harris seemed to be having nothing. Nina's immediate impulse was to have a double of anything, considering the circumstances.

"I have an open bottle of chardonnay, if you'd like some," Marilyn suggested.

It would have been rude to say "Keep your wine, I'll have four fingers of Southern Comfort, thank you very much." So Nina just said, "That'll be fine," and accepted the glass.

Nina wondered why that wine was already open. Did Marilyn Harris spend her days in the kitchen, chopping figs and tippling? Nina had grown up in the kind of house where there was never an open bottle of wine. She doubted whether Ida Fischman even knew how to operate a corkscrew.

"Would you like an olive?" Marilyn held up a small but heavy crystal dish.

"Thank you." Nor did Nina grow up in a house where there were bowls of olives. There had been a jar of the ones stuffed with pimientos at the back of a refrigerator shelf, probably the same jar throughout her childhood. She had never seen her mother touch an olive with any more frequency than she had seen her pick up a corkscrew.

Chopped liver was the only hors d'oeuvre ever served in the Fischman household. It had been served on slices of rye bread cut into halves. But when Guttman's, the neighborhood Jewish bakery, closed and reopened as a pizza parlor, Ida switched to Ritz crackers without showing any deep regret. She continued, however, to use only real chicken schmaltz in her recipe, dutifully skimming the pan whenever she put a roaster in the oven, and pouring the fat into a stash she kept in the freezer. Nina wondered when Marilyn had made the switch from chopped liver to olives. Because she just couldn't believe that someone with such big floppy earlobes had grown up eating olives out of Baccarat pickle dishes.

"Nina, Jonathan tells me you prefer New York to California," Marilyn said.

Nina didn't know how to respond. She felt like she was on a white-water rafting trip. On the left riverbank was Marilyn's feeling that someone like Nina had no right to dare to leave Jonathan. On the right bank was Marilyn's probable relief that he had escaped Nina's clutches. And straight ahead of her were the rapids—if you left him, what the hell are you doing here in my house?

"I did not do well in Los Angeles," Nina said, as noncommittal an answer as she could think of.

"So you're an attorney," Norman said. "Did you take the bar while you were out there?"

Nina considered telling Norman Harris about how she could barely change her Tampax out there, much less study for the California bar exam. But she knew he wouldn't be a receptive audience. Guys of his particular ethnic and age group only talked about business, until they developed cardiac problems. Then they discussed their cholesterol and triglycerides as if they were analyzing a profit-and-loss statement.

"No, we got there too late for the summer exam and I didn't stick around long enough for the winter one." They used to make her feel like such a failure, that generation of Jewish fathers, when she would try to explain why she worked for a federally funded poverty program instead of having a real practice with real clients. And now that she wasn't even working, she was starting to have trouble even staying in the same room with this guy.

Her father had had the same trouble. At a time when his contemporaries were expanding their businesses and hiring accountants and moving to the suburbs, Leo Fischman was somehow missing the boat. And it hadn't been an era when you could charmingly explain about how your shrink thought you had success anxiety due to early childhood trauma. If you weren't making money, you were shit. And that was that. "How ya doing?" men would ask him, and he'd know what they meant.

Nina sometimes felt caught in the same trap. Her entire life she had been judged on how thin she was, or how many children she had, or how much money she made. All losing propositions. But the good thing was that women these days were judged on so many things, when you were looking really pathetic you could always switch arenas. Turn the conversation around to the five pounds you just lost or the appeal you just won. Leo Fischman had not had any such luxury.

Guys like Norman Harris always made Nina defensive, brought her right back to those sad times when she would watch her father flinch in the temple parking lot. Dreading to go in and thrust himself into the crowd that swarmed whatever bar mitzvah or wedding the Fischmans had been invited to. The crowd that lay in wait for Leo Fischman, anxious to ask "How ya doing?"

Even though Norman Harris made her feel like a crummy little failure, Nina didn't really miss working. Stuck in L.A. she had desperately missed her job, or so she had thought. But back in New York, on her own turf, she realized she had been wrong. It had been New York she missed, not the daily grind of practicing law. In fact, now that she had some distance, it was even clearer what an unnatural and desiccated system the law was. Nina liked her current luxury of being able to say what she meant for no reason other than her desire to convey an idea. She could go on like this forever.

"What do you plan on doing?" Marilyn Harris asked her. Nina knew that she didn't mean *doing* as Norman would, as in doing for a living. Mrs. Harris meant it in both the vaguest and most specific ways—doing with your life, doing with your hair, doing with your rapidly failing ovaries. Maybe Norman Harris was the kind of guy who could have made Leo Fischman feel like shit, but Nina knew it was Marilyn who was the one for her to watch in this particular situation.

Nina pulled out her trump card. "Oh, I'm writing for *The New Yorker*." She sat back and watched the heads snap to attention. Including Jonathan's. She hadn't told him in the car on the way over, preferring to save it for when she really needed it. "Well, researching more than writing. Helping an old friend with an exhaustive piece on local politics. Have any of you ever heard of Ellen Simon?"

"The one who left her husband?" Marilyn asked.

Poor Ellen. She had spent every moment of her life trying to be famous. Ellen Simon had been the kind of kid who probably sent out press releases when she was toilet trained. And ultimately this was what she was known for—dumping her husband.

"That's Ellen. In addition to her syndicated column, she's also freelancing for *The New Yorker*."

"Yes, the magazine has changed, hasn't it." Marilyn pursed her lips just a bit.

Good one, Nina thought. You've managed to insult a writer, an editor, and a magazine with just a few syllables and a subtle facial expression. Not to mention that Nina didn't have to be terribly paranoid to be slightly insulted herself. An expert insult artist, that Marilyn Harris.

"What are you researching?" Marilyn asked, pronouncing the word with distaste, as if Nina were rummaging instead of researching.

"I'm looking into some allegations about the Brooklyn D.A. A cover-up in a murder investigation."

"Ed Daley? I know his wife," Marilyn said.

"You do?"

"Yes, Dottie and I have done some charity work together."

"Really?" Could Marilyn be a member of SPASM? The woman didn't look like she was too fond of any mammals, either small or large. In fact, she hadn't even so much as looked at her own son since he had entered the house.

"Actually," Nina said, "I met Dottie just a few days ago. What kind of charity work were you involved in?"

"A beautification program. Some joint landscaping program between Brooklyn and Queens."

"She's into annuals in a big way, isn't she?" Nina said, proud of herself for being able to make a gardening joke.

"She's into a lot of things."

"What do you mean?"

"Dottie's got a lot of . . . umm . . . energy. To say the least. She once told me this amazing story about how she infiltrated this voodoo sect."

"Voodoo?"

"Yeah. Did you ever hear of candomblé?"

"No, what's that?"

"Some kind of voodoo worship they have in Brazil. There were a bunch of people in Brooklyn practicing ritual animal sacrifice. I don't know if you're aware of this, but Dottie's very active in the animal rights movement."

"Yeah, I know."

"She claimed that she got them to take her in as a member. Can you imagine? A big strawberry blonde like her running around with a bunch of South Americans?" Marilyn made it seem as though only her coloring was wrong.

"It must have been quite something."

"I think she ended up being a little more enthusiastic about the cult than she admitted. As if she secretly wanted to practice voodoo."

Nina could almost see it. Dottie Daley was a woman of

great enthusiasms. It wasn't that hard to imagine her swaddling herself in white *schmattas* and slitting the throats of a few sheep and goats in some garage in Sunset Park. It was easier to picture her practicing voodoo than sitting on the board of some gardening project.

"Did she actually kill animals?" Nina asked.

"I bet she did."

"How could she?"

"She's a woman of vast contradictions," Marilyn said.

"Like Nina," Jonathan said.

Nina realized that those were the first words he had uttered since walking through the door.

CHAPTER
FOURTEEN

"You did great," Jonathan said in the car, while driving her home.

"I don't know," she said. "I mean, I don't think that either of them actually liked me."

"Well, my mother liked your hair. That's more positive than she feels about most people."

"Yeah, she's a pretty tough customer. So's Norman."

"He is. Now you know why I had to move all the way to California."

"I didn't think that was your idea," Nina said, much too sharply.

"It wasn't originally. But I must admit, I'm getting very comfortable in L.A."

Probably even more so, Nina thought, now that you don't have me on your couch, kvetching and whining.

"I guess," he continued, "it has something to do with the fact that not every guy out there in a suit reminds me of my father. The way they do in New York. Not that the California crowd is any better. You can't find a single vent in all the suits in Los Angeles County. And there's enough gel in their hair to slick back the coats of an entire herd of Angora goats."

"That's funny, but it doesn't sound like something Jonathan Harris would say."

"Yeah, well it's something I heard on television. Jesus, I

can't get anything past you. Have you been taking lessons from my mother?"

Nina let the accusation drop. She supposed that she was a little like his mother, insofar as they could probably both tell when he was stealing jokes, since they both knew him really well. That was the reason people gave for maintaining old friendships. "You really know me," men had told her after they dumped her. "I hope we can be friends."

She had never wanted to. Those relationships were like books she had finished reading. They were over, now on to something new. As if on cue, Jonathan said, "Even though I'm flying back on Saturday, I hope we stay in touch."

"Why?" She never had the nerve to ask that before. But what the hell, she had already decided she had nothing left to lose.

"Why?" he repeated, clearly shocked.

"Yeah, why? Why do you still want us to be friends? You're in California, I'm in New York, I practically had a nervous breakdown on your living room couch and then I flew home to my mother. Why do you still want to have anything to do with me, anyway?"

"Because you understand me."

Nina considered this carefully. Perhaps, she thought, men were always looking for women to understand them, in hope that the women's understanding would nurture and protect them. Women, on the other hand, were afraid of those men who understood them, because it made the women more vulnerable and gave the men more power.

"Besides," Jonathan continued, "we have history."

"Yeah, well, the Third Reich had history too. That doesn't mean it should continue to exist."

"Is that how you think of our relationship? As the Third Reich?"

"I'm sorry I said that. I didn't really mean it."

"I miss you." He took his right hand off the steering wheel and gave her neck a squeeze.

It suddenly occurred to Nina that Jonathan might want to get laid. He wasn't the kind of guy who came roaring through the door, his hand fumbling with his zipper, determined to have his way with you. But he did make his needs known from time to time and unless Nina was in the middle of something important, like eating Chinese food or watching *Seinfeld*, she accommodated him.

She had also noticed that it wasn't always reciprocated. But she didn't push it, since she found that when he was urged to turn off the computer and put down the magazine and come to bed, his performance level suffered, making the entire enterprise barely worthwhile.

But what the hell was she supposed to do, here on the Grand Central Parkway, on the way to her mother's apartment? Pull over and check into the Holiday Inn next to LaGuardia Airport? She was certainly not about to invite him to stay over at her mother's house, not after she had gone on and on to Ida about how it was all over. And it was all over, wasn't it? Hadn't she just been telling herself about books she had finished reading and all?

But she hated to turn down the opportunity. Nina shared the prejudice of her generation that sexual activity was a healthy thing, something you should do frequently, like getting your teeth cleaned. If the interval between the acts got too long, you could develop some sort of corrosive buildup.

People who came of age in the fifties, those ten years older than Nina, still believed in sex as something holy. The illicit nature of the act never lost its grip on their imaginations, and as a result they still went to Freudian shrinks to talk about it at a hundred dollars an hour and occasionally did weird things about it, like Woody Allen.

The ones ten years younger than Nina had, at an early age, seen the ruinous decay that rampant promiscuity could wreak. They were naturally cautious, preferring instead to put notches in their belts for job promotions and for marrying people who had rich fathers.

It wasn't always as easy to schedule as getting your teeth cleaned, however, so the tendency to binge and hoard was hard to avoid. Nina looked out past the windshield, down the Grand Central Parkway, and watched a long dry spell coming up over the horizon. Jesus, she told herself, sex wasn't something you could store up, like nuts in a squirrel's cheeks. They could probably find a place to go. Laura had switched the dinner from Westhampton to Brooklyn, but Ida might still be staying over. They could have the place to themselves, but what would be the point?

"Do you miss me at all?" he asked.

She started to answer in several different ways: I miss certain things about you. I miss our life together. I miss you, but I'm glad not to be living with you in California. But it all sounded so clinical, like a contrived answer to a trick question on a test.

"Not really," she finally said.

He pouted, of course. But she figured that he wasn't the kind of guy who would drive the car off the road.

There was still one thing she didn't understand. Go for it, she told herself, freedom's just another word for nothing left to lose.

"Jonathan, can I ask you a question?"

"I guess so."

"I still don't understand why, at this terminal stage in the game, you finally decided to introduce me to your parents."

"Um, I guess I wanted to show you off."

"Now? Now that we're not together anymore? Does that make any sense?"

"I don't know," he mumbled, without taking his eyes off the road. "Actually, I kinda led them to believe that we were probably planning to get back together."

"Why did you tell them that?"

"Because I thought we might. After you left, I expected you to come walking back through the door any minute."

"You did?" Only men could be so pathetic and arrogant at the same time. "Well, I'm not going to, you know," she said.

"Yeah, I know."

"So you might as well tell your parents the truth."

"My parents are the least of my problems."

Somehow Nina didn't think so.

CHAPTER FIFTEEN

IDA WAS STILL UP, watching *Letterman*.

"Did Ken drive you back from Brooklyn?" Nina asked her mother.

"Yeah, he's got some kind of monthly parking space now, so he doesn't get hysterical anymore when Laura tells him to take me home. It used to be so bad that every time I walked in the door, his face would fall in anticipation of losing his parking spot. Really, I've never seen such a change in a person."

"How was the food?"

"Terrific. The same as always."

"She's still doing the turkey with the dried cherries?" Laura had always been a *Silver Palate* devotee. The two authors with their overambitious ingredients somehow made Nina's sister feel as though her existence was justified. The preparation methods were simple, but you had to visit several esoteric stores in order to get started. The books were really written for people who preferred shopping to cooking. When their compendium volume, *The New Basics*, came out several years ago, the Thanksgiving turkey recipe included dried cherries, an ingredient that apparently had not yet made its way from the Upper Peninsula of Michigan to the gourmet boutiques of New York City.

Laura had scoured Park Slope and Manhattan without

any success. She described the scene at Zabar's to Nina, where a dozen haunted and pinched faces harassed the help, pleading for dried cherries. The zeitgeist had struck and the Zabar family had fallen behind. Some people substituted dried apricots that year, others tried currants. Laura resorted to her previous year's recipe, which featured some kind of complicated glaze. By the following November dried cherries were on every corner, but Laura, never having recovered from the original dried cherry shortage, kept an ample supply in her pantry, just in case.

"Dried cherries? I guess so," Ida said. "I wasn't really paying attention." Like many women of her generation, Ida considered cooking to be up there with cleaning bathrooms and ironing shirts in terms of glamor. She never understood why it was listed in course catalogs along with underwater photography and stress reduction. As far as Ida was concerned, cooking was the opposite of stress reduction.

"How was the food at yours?" Ida asked.

"The food? Okay." It wasn't the question Nina had expected. But Nina should have known that it was only a warm-up.

"And the ambiance?"

"Hmmm. Where do I start?" Nina was grateful for Ida's presence, providing a ready-made audience for her daughter's freshly minted observations. Moving back into your mother's house, aside from being a totally humiliating experience, did have some of the fun qualities of a nonstop pajama party.

"Their names are Marilyn and Norman. Probably straddling seventy, a little younger than you. Definitely less of a Depression mentality. Believe me, these two never had to agonize over whether or not to join the Communist Party."

"*Yekkes?*" It was an antiquated term, what the non-

German Jews had called their German brethren back in
the thirties, when the refugees flooded Manhattan. The
word contained more contempt than awe. *Yekke* was the
Yiddish term for "jacket." Not only did the Germans wear
them, but they kept them buttoned up.

"I don't think they're German. I don't know why, but I
sensed a faint Eastern European background popping up
through the classy patina. Some sort of Polish penti-
mento."

"Can you be more specific?"

That was one of the best things about her mother.
When Nina went off on one of her far-fetched digres-
sions, Ida always asked her to be more specific and never
rolled her eyes.

"Let's see." Nina avoided the floppy earlobes and
lumpy legs. She was trying for something more imaginative. "I guess it was their accents. Not that they dropped
their *r*'s or dentalized their *t*'s or anything terribly obvious. But she referred to *Hamlet* once and I swear she
pronounced it 'Haymlet.' Very boroughy. If they're German, they're not the Temple Emanu-El types."

"Fat or thin?" Ida asked.

Nina knew she meant Marilyn. "Not thin, but contained." Nina, if asked, could not explain how she could
tell if someone was naturally thin or watched themselves
like a hawk. But she had a pretty good track record.

"Was she nice to you?"

"I'll give you some idea. At one point, I was standing
across the room, she looked me up and down and said,
'You have a good head of hair.' Now, does that qualify as
nice?"

"It depends. Did she look you up and down just to the
waist? Or all the way down?"

"To my toenails."

"That wasn't nice. What about Norman?"

"Ah, he's one of those guys who just doesn't play well outside the office. At work they seem sharp and in control, but at home they just seem mean and boring."

"What does he do?"

"Some kind of business that he inherited from his father. Raincoats, I think. Although he's not your typical gold chain garmento."

"There's one thing I don't understand," Ida said.

"What's that?"

"You move to California with this guy, but you don't know where his parents grew up or what business his family is in. Nina, that's not like you. What's the story?"

"It's odd, isn't it? But every time the conversation would come around to his parents, Jonathan's jaw would jut out in this tense way and this muscle would start twitching just at the point where his mandible is attached to his head. And it gave me a pretty clear idea that it would be unwise to pry. So I never asked him anything. I let him take the conversational lead."

"Really?"

"Why are you so surprised? Don't you think I'm capable of verbal deference? I read all those women's magazines when I was younger. I know how to talk to men."

"Okay, I believe you. I'm sure you have many talents that I'm unaware of. So what did you say to him this time?"

"What do you mean?"

"You just told me that you know how to talk to men. What did you tell Jonathan?"

"What makes you think that I told him anything?"

"I can just tell. I see the aftermath of a pivotal conversation written all over your face."

"Oh, okay." This was no longer feeling like a fun pajama party. "I told him that it was over and there was no point in trying to be friends."

"That sounds sensible."

"It does?"

"Well, is that the way you feel?"

"Yeah, it is."

"So you might as well tell him so."

"I guess you're right." It seemed so much simpler here in her mother's living room than it had on the Grand Central Parkway. A short and swift epilogue to another finished book. Maybe.

"How did he take it?"

"Okay, I guess." Nina fished around for a change of subject. "You know, Marilyn claimed to know Dottie Daley. The district attorney's wife."

"She did? How come? I don't see those two running in the same circles."

"No, it seems unlikely. But they had done some volunteer work together. It's funny, really, to think that Dottie's married to a chief law enforcement officer. She seems like a natural-born outlaw."

"Opposites attract."

"Maybe. Marilyn said Dottie told her that she got all involved in some Brazilian voodoo sect in Brooklyn. That she infiltrated them in order to investigate their animal sacrificial rites."

"Candomblé?" Ida asked.

"How did you know?"

"Don't you read Jorge Amado?"

"No, though I've tried." Nina loved the idea of South American literature and would have been a big fan. However, mystic surrealism and its lyric meanderings were so antithetical to Nina's life, spent in nonmystical, very real places like housing court, that she never got past the first few chapters. Now that she was unemployed and her life was more surreal, maybe she'd give the genre another try. But she'd take a stab at Isabel Allende before she'd go back to Jorge Amado. Sisterhood was still, after all these years, at least a little bit powerful.

"How do you have the patience for that stuff?" she asked her mother.

"Where am I rushing to?" Actually, Ida read everything. Like most children of immigrants, Ida considered reading as a way to understand the world, to gain entry into places that were out of her reach. The farther the better.

Her daughter had left the book as frigate concept behind. Nina tended to search out the latest author that reminded her of herself. Rushing from one place to another, she indulged her impulse to use books to reassure herself that women like Nina were still desirable, still had something to say, that people still wanted to listen to them.

"So what does Jorge Amado have to say about candomblé?" Nina asked.

"It's very big in Bahia, the province in Brazil with the most African influence. It was where they shipped all the slaves. And after all these centuries, candomblé is still giving the Catholic Church a run for its money. Amazing, isn't it, how so many of these old, quirky religions with the eccentric rituals just will not die out."

"Yeah, like Judaism. At least voodoo practitioners wear nice comfortable cottons instead of heavy black woolen suits that you could *schvitz* to death in," Nina said. "So are they into slaughtering animals?"

"Goats, chickens, the usual."

"Any human sacrifices?"

"I don't know. Why?"

"Maybe Dottie Daley got really whacked out on candomblé and killed Andy Campbell in a murderous rage. And now her husband is covering it up."

"Doesn't sound too likely to me," Ida said. "Now,

where did you hear all this about the D.A.'s office dropping this investigation? Was it just from Roz? Or did someone else confirm it?"

"Let me think. No, it was just Roz."

"And where did she hear it from?"

"I don't think that she specified. You were there, Ma. Do you remember?"

"She just said that she had heard it somewhere. She didn't give any details. You should go back and have another conversation with her, don't you think?"

"Yeah, I'll call her tomorrow."

Letterman was saying good night. It was time to do the same. Nina wondered how many more nights would be like this, staying up late, sleeping in, drifting along. This was like an open-ended college vacation, without the marijuana. Life could be worse.

CHAPTER
SIXTEEN

NINA CAUGHT UP with Roz the next day, but not until late in the afternoon. "I'm sorry I missed your calls," Roz said, "but I've been frantic."

"What's wrong?" Or was that a stupid thing to ask someone whose husband had recently been murdered?

"Oh, I'm doing a big bridal party in D.C. It's in two weeks and it's been impossible to schedule everyone's fittings. This is the absolute last time I ever take on any out-of-town work." Roz sounded breathless, but in a glamorous way. As if her out-of-town work was opening night in New Haven, instead of measuring a bunch of JAP-py heads in Silver Spring.

"The reason I called," Nina said, "was to discuss something you mentioned last time we met."

"And what was that?"

"About the Brooklyn D.A.'s office."

"What about it?" Nina couldn't decipher the odd tone in Roz's voice. It wasn't exactly defensive. *Mocking* might be a more accurate description.

"You presented a theory about a cover-up. You said that Daley's office wasn't investigating the possibility that Andy had been killed by animal rights activists. And you blamed it on his wife's involvement in the movement."

"Yeah, well, now I'm not so sure." Roz sounded apologetic, but only the tiniest bit.

"What do you mean?" Nina asked.

"Actually, I got a call from the D.A.'s office. An investigator named Fallon. He asked me a few questions, so I asked him a few questions. And he pretty much convinced me that they're doing a pretty thorough job. I even talked to Peter Slater."

"You did?"

"Yeah. After your conversation with him, he apparently talked to the more activist membership to make sure they were all clean. He seemed very concerned."

Concerned? Thorough? These were not words that a woman like Roz used. No New Yorkers used them very often. Nobody was ever happy with the job anyone was doing, never satisfied with the response that they got. Kvetching was a noble local art form, occasionally elevated in stature with a fancy name like consumer advocate.

And Nina was absolutely sure that Roz Brillstein was an experienced practitioner. A natural-born critic. She had the shrewd, watchful eye of someone who knows her way around the complaint department.

Why was Roz rolling over and playing dead when it came to something as important as her husband's murder? Something screwy was going on here, but Roz was a hard one to read. Her subtext was even thicker than her hair.

"What made you suspect the animal rights people in the first place?" Nina asked.

"Well, it makes sense. It seems obvious, in light of all those threats that they used to get at work."

"Did Andy complain a lot?"

"Oh, no. He really only mentioned once, ages ago, that someone had spray-painted graffiti in the lab."

"What did it say?"

"Stop the killing, I think. Frankly, it was so long ago that I don't remember."

"And then?"

"And then he never mentioned it again. And I never would have known anything was going on if I hadn't gone to a staff party. Almost everyone who worked in the lab was there. And it was right around the time when one of those abortion doctors was killed. And a bunch of Andy's colleagues got into a discussion of who was crazier—the fetus people or the animal people. Later someone told me about all the threats they'd gotten over the years. Well, I had no idea. It really freaked me out."

"Why, do you think, was Andy so close-mouthed about it?"

"He liked to downplay things."

Nina could imagine. Andy and Roz were straight out of central casting—the calm, blond WASP and the dark, volatile Jew. Perhaps Roz had married him simply because he played such perfect counterpoint to her. Andy made her look more colorful, more tragic, more vibrant, more everything.

"I guess I got pretty upset," Roz continued, "that first time with the graffiti. In fact, I started having the worst nightmares. Rats escaping from their cages and eating his face off, that kind of thing. Andy sheltered me from a lot. And what am I going to do now?"

If you have a nervous breakdown, Nina thought, *I'm sure you'll do it with a great deal of style.*

"You know, sometimes people polarize each other," Nina said. "If Andy was the one who always minimized the situation, you never had to. Now that he's gone, it's up to you to be calm and rational. At least for the kids."

"Who the hell do you think you are? Dr. Joyce Brothers?"

Nina never counted herself as one of the more insuffer-

able people in the world. There was so much competition. But she was, after all, a schoolteacher's daughter.
And every now and then she'd suffer a minor stroke and
display such severe didactic tendencies that someone
would have to ask her who the hell she thought she was.

"Yeah, what do I know?" Nina said. "I haven't been
able to sustain a relationship past its first anniversary."

"You know what you should do?" Roz said.

"Keep my fat trap shut?"

"Color your hair."

Here was a woman who was struggling with the exigen-
cies of recent widowhood, coping with two children who
had just lost their father. Yet she was able to focus on the
little bit of gray that Nina told herself nobody noticed.
"Do you really think so?" she asked Roz.

"Absolutely. You've got nice, high color—pink cheeks,
blue eyes. But your hair is drabbing it all out."

"The guy who cuts it keeps telling me to put highlights
in it. What do you think?"

"Too trite. Everybody with light brown hair automati-
cally thinks blond. If you lived on Long Island, I'd say go
with highlights. But if I were you, I'd go darker. Your
coloring is strong enough to carry it. And your eyebrows
are definitely those of a brunette."

How grief stricken could Roz be if she remembered the
color of Nina's eyebrows, for chrissakes? And it seemed
strange to Nina how all of a sudden Roz was backpedaling
on her previous accusations.

"What did you think of Peter Slater?" Nina asked.

"Cute."

"Cute? You mean you met him? I thought you said you
spoke with him."

"I did."

"But not on the phone?"

"Well, first I spoke with him on the phone, and then I met him."

"Really. Well, what assurances did he give you that no one in his organization had been involved?"

"He really did look into it. Peter admitted that several of the members of AFTA did threaten researchers. Not only at Morgan, but also up at Columbia-Presbyterian. So he talked to them, and they had all been out of town at some crackpot convention in Texas the week that Andy died."

"Very convenient."

"Well," Roz said, "Peter sounded like he was telling me the truth."

"He's the kind of guy where it's hard to tell if they're lying. They tell everything so well—both the truth and lies. Like a high-priced lawyer."

"I found him to be sincere."

"Do you think he's gay?"

Roz paused a good while. "I think that Peter," she finally said, "is one of those people who doesn't necessarily confine himself to any one category of partner."

Well, Nina thought, that was a nicer way of putting it than saying that the man would fuck a knothole in a tree.

"Peter is expansive," Roz said, "in the truest sense of the word."

What did that mean? Nina wondered. That his cock got really big when it got hard? And Roz was throwing his name around a lot, slipping it into every sentence. Was she sleeping with him? Nina knew that any exploration of this particular theme must be approached with caution. Where should she start?

"Umm, do you think—"

Roz cut her off. "Nina," she said. "Do me one favor. Please?"

"What's that?"

"I'm going to give you the phone number of my color-ist. Call him. Don't put it off, because he's going away for a month around Christmas."

"Gee, I don't know."

"You'll be amazed what a difference it will make in your life. You'll walk faster, your skin will be clearer, even your boobs will sag less."

"Maybe I should just get a breast lift."

"I have a phone number for that too," Roz said. "But start with the hair. You can move on later. Trust me."

Had Roz had her tits done? Had Peter Slater gotten his hands on them? Maybe Roz and Peter had been lovers all along, and they bumped Andy off, using the animal rights movement as camouflage. But if that was true, why had Roz accused him in the first place?

Roz Brillstein was a complicated woman, capable of God knew what. But one thing was definite—she had great hair.

CHAPTER SEVENTEEN

ROZ'S COLORIST'S NAME was Hector. He was Puerto Rican, but had green eyes and blond hair. The eyes were natural, the hair was not. But the look worked. Actually, he inspired confidence. Nina figured that any guy who could pull off being a blond Puerto Rican had to know what he was doing.

As it turned out, Hector had grown up in the same neighborhood as Nina and had attended the same junior high school, although she had a few years on him. He worked in a small shop in the Village. Nina nervously wondered what the proper etiquette was in the world of hair coloring—did you have to get it cut in the same place as you got it colored? Did Hector also cut hair? If so, would he resent hair that had been cut by someone else and perhaps take it out on Nina's head?

An experienced friend had assured Nina that it was perfectly acceptable to have the two services performed in different places. In fact, it was akin to being a smart shopper. It showed that you were discerning, a woman who knew enough to go to a specialist.

"So, how do you know Roz?" he asked, while inspecting the gray strands that peppered the top of Nina's head.

"She's a friend of my sister's."

"Do I know your sister?"

"I don't know. Her name is Laura Rubin. She doesn't

color her hair. And I'm not sure where she gets it cut. Do you cut hair too?" It seemed a convenient way to find out.

"No, just color. I used to, but I prefer color. And I've got enough clients now that I don't have to cut anymore."

"Oh. Well, my sister's got the kind of dark hair that looks better the grayer it gets. You know what I mean?"

"Just slowly turns silver."

"Right. While mine used to be pretty light and now it just gets drabber and drabber. She also has the kind of thighs that just get thinner and thinner, but we don't have to get into that now."

He smiled. "What were you thinking of?"

It was too hard a question to answer.

"In terms of color," he added, when he saw that Nina seemed confused.

"I don't know. The guy who cuts it is always telling me to put highlights in. Honey highlights, he keeps saying."

"I don't know how much coverage you're going to get from highlights. There's a lot of gray here."

Nina sighed. "I suppose there is. I don't know, what do you suggest?"

"How would you feel about being a brunette?" Hector asked.

"You know, after living in southern California for a while, I'd feel terrific about being a brunette."

She realized after she said it that Hector the blond might be offended. But he didn't seem to take it personally. He showed her a swatch of some color that really could only be described as brown. It would be the end of an era, of being an almost blond, or a dark blond or a Jewish blond or a polychromatic blond, or any of the other silly descriptions she'd used over the years. Nina was going to have brown hair.

"Let's do it," she said.

Hector sent her over to be washed as he mixed up a batch of paste. As he carefully painted her head with it, she slid the conversation around to Roz Brillstein.

"How much red is it going to have?" she asked.

"A little."

"How much compared to Roz?"

"No, nothing like that. To get away with that burgundy look, you need brown eyes. Otherwise you can end up looking like an American flag."

"A flag?"

"You know, red, white, and blue."

"Well, I don't want to look like a flag. She's got a great look, I think. Very dramatic."

"You think that Roz looks dramatic now," said Hector, "you should have seen her before she got married."

"How long have you known her?"

"About fifteen years. We both used to live on the Lower East Side. I was working in a shop on St. Marks Place when we met. She used to keep her hair very black, in a china-doll's cut, with white face makeup and a lot of kohl around the eyes."

"Oh, yeah. I remember kohl. Everyone was using it after they got back from Morocco. I tried it for a while, but I was never fully convinced that it wasn't blinding me."

"Well, Roz was very into that Kabuki look. She used something on her lips that made them very red, but with a totally matte finish. I always wondered what it was, but I could never get her to tell me."

"Isn't that silly? I can never understand it when someone won't share a recipe or tell you the gender results of their amniocentesis. Why keep your brand of lipstick a secret, for chrissakes?"

"With some people I think it's a part of themselves that they don't want to share."

"But lipstick? What part of Roz did lipstick represent?"

"She probably thought she was cultivating an air of mystery," Hector said.

"Now, *that* I've never even remotely understood. Mystery is a language I've never learned to speak."

"Well, Roz used to have a lot of secrets. I think they made her feel powerful."

"And now?"

"Now things are different." Hector paused. But the great thing about cross-examining your colorist was that he couldn't just walk out of the room. He had to stand there, brushing paste onto your hair and answering your questions.

"Different in what way?" Nina asked.

"Roz was so dramatic back then, especially when it came to her secrets. She'd always flaunt them, playing them like . . . uh . . . *como se dice* . . . ?"

"A poker hand?"

"Yeah. Revealing them slowly, one by one, for the greatest dramatic effect."

"What kind of secrets?"

"It was a time of great sexual drama. For all of us. But particularly for Roz."

Nina took a calculated risk. "Were you ever sexually involved with her?"

Hector's green eyes narrowed. "Me? No. But several of my friends were. Really, these kids on college campuses think that they invented bisexuality. But back then you couldn't even have tried to chart all the comings and going that went on between Avenues A and D."

"Did Roz have a weakness for bisexual men?"

"Not in particular. It was just that she couldn't resist a

good-looking man. And if he was a little . . . umm . . . disoriented, she wasn't going to let that put her off."

"And all this stopped when she married Andy?"

"She struggled with it. It was very hard for her to make the adjustment."

"You mean she cheated on him?"

"I imagine so."

"All along?"

"No, I think she stopped once her son was born." He dabbed some paste from her ear.

"I've never heard of anyone else naming a kid Wolf."

"She had an uncle named Wolf who never made it out of Europe. She tells people that her son is named after him, but that's not really it."

"What's the real story?"

"While she was pregnant she went out to Minnesota to study with some Native American tribe. And part of the trip was that they revealed your power animal to you."

"And hers was a wolf?"

"Right. Although she wasn't supposed to tell anyone. So she named her kid Wolf instead."

"And Andy put up with all this? A pregnant wife running off to Minnesota and then naming their firstborn son after her power animal?"

"I guess so. Nina, I'm going to let you sit for thirty minutes. Then we'll see what you look like." Hector picked up a kitchen timer and set it for thirty minutes. "Why don't you sit over there," he said.

"Okay." Nina was tired of staring at herself in the mirror and happy to move to a chair facing the wall. But she hadn't gotten enough of the saga of Roz Brillstein. She had really hit the mother lode with Hector. It wasn't much of a surprise. Hair stylists were to women what bartenders were to men. If you didn't have a good narrative line, it barely mattered what brilliant effects you achieved on top of people's heads.

Nina spent the next thirty minutes reading *OUT!* magazine, which had been lying on the table next to *Vanity Fair*. She found it very refreshing to read interviews with people who didn't have to pretend they were straight. She wondered whether anyone would ever get around to publishing *FAT!* magazine.

The timer went off. A young woman with a pierced nostril washed out Nina's hair and returned her to Hector's chair.

"What do you think?" he asked.

"It's brown."

"Let me dry it for you. It won't look as dark."

"Okay." Nina waited until he had put the diffusing attachment onto the blow dryer. "Now, you were right in the middle of telling me how come Andy let Roz get away with all of her carrying on."

"I was?" Hector thought about it for a minute. "Andy worshipped her," he said. "He was convinced that she was the best thing that ever happened to him. That without Roz he'd be just some boring science nerd."

"Really? How do you get some man to think that about you?" Nina asked.

"Sex. She had an amazing sexual hold on him. He never stopped drooling over her."

"Was it mutual?"

"Hardly."

"So what did she see in him? He wasn't rich, he wasn't powerful. I've heard that he had a brilliant mind for scientific research, but I somehow don't think that was Roz's thing."

"I don't know," Hector said. "Why do Jewish men marry shiksas?"

It was reassuring to Nina that she was having her hair

colored by a Puerto Rican who knew some Yiddish. "They want to have children with long, thin limbs and blond hair so that the Nazis won't get them?" she proposed.

"I'm sure that the Nazis were on Roz's mind when she married Andy. They were always on her mind."

"So he was really hot for her, huh?" Nina said. "And she didn't feel the same way about him. That can get on your nerves after a while. I suppose all that sexual power can be wearing. I wouldn't know."

Hector put down the blow dryer and spun her around in the chair. "So what do you think?" he asked.

It was a rich shade of brown, with enough red in it to add visual interest. Maybe now she would be able to wear khaki. She definitely looked more youthful, but she looked more something else too. What was it? Dramatic? Powerful? Serious? No, that wasn't it. "I like it," she said. "I like it a lot." Her voice sounded lower. Was that possible? And then it struck her. Her new hair color made her look more Jewish. And it also struck her that looking more Jewish was fine with her.

CHAPTER
EIGHTEEN

IDA DIDN'T NOTICE Nina's hair. It made Nina wonder how a woman who could spot a missing comma in a two-hundred-thousand-word manuscript could be absolutely blind when it came to personal appearances.

Ida had her own set of fashion tips, including: *Don't like what you see in the mirror? Put on a string of amethyst beads. They'll make you feel better.* She was the kind of woman who regretted that New Balance didn't make any of their running shoes in purple. Every now and then she'd have a flash of sheer brilliance—an embroidered bathrobe or a batik scarf or a carved jade pendant would be just the most beautiful thing you'd ever seen. But most of the time Ida was oblivious. Maybe if Nina had dyed her hair purple, her mother would have noticed.

"Where were you?" Ida asked.

"Getting my hair colored."

"Oh, very nice. Did you cut it too?"

"No."

"It looks shorter."

"Ma, you're an idiot. But also a genius. Tell me what you think of this."

"Of what?"

"Well, the guy who colored my hair has known Roz for about fifteen years."

"Really?"

"Actually, she recommended him. So it's not really that much of a coincidence."

"Am I to assume that he gave you some really good gossip?"

"How did you know?" Nina asked.

"I could tell by the look on your face."

"You mean to tell me that you can tell what I'm thinking by the merest tightening of a facial muscle. Yet you had no idea that your daughter was a brunette for the first time in her life, even though she was standing right in front of you."

"What do you mean? Your hair was always brown."

"Light brown, maybe. But not brown brown."

"Yeah, it looks a little darker, now that you mention it."

Nina considered launching into a lengthy explanation of how totally different she felt with her new hair color. How she now strode instead of walked, how she bellowed instead of squeaked. But now it all seemed so silly, like she had imagined all the striding and bellowing. For about the millionth time in her life, she wished that she had a mother who could make her feel that a shade or two difference in hair color was the most important thing in the world. But then she remembered all the things that went along with mothers like that. She thought of all the women she knew who had monthly bikini waxes and zapped every spider vein with lasers and spent thousands of dollars and hundreds of hours on contact lenses and cosmetic surgery. She should never forget that a little obliviousness in a mother could be a good thing.

"So what did he tell you about Roz?" Ida asked.

Nina allowed herself to sneak a final peek at her hair in the reflection of the tea kettle before she set her priorities straight and settled into a kitchen chair.

"I think she used to cheat on Andy," Nina said.

"What a surprise."

"This guy Hector said that she rode a pretty wide circuit, including some of his friends. And I would hazard a
guess that his friends are not exactly golf playing, Scotch
drinking, red-blooded American men." Nina paused to
wonder whether there were golf courses that catered to
gay men. If not, it might prove to be a lucrative business
venture.

"How many golf players have you gone out with in your
time?" Ida asked her.

"Probably none. How about you?"

"I can't think of any. But it's less likely for me. Jews
didn't start playing golf until I was off the market. In fact,
they were just picking up their first tennis racquets about
the time I got married."

"Assimilation spreads rapidly."

"Like gypsy moths."

"You could have gone out with a golf player after
Daddy died," Nina pointed out.

"I could have. But I haven't been riding a very wide
circuit myself."

No one really expected Ida Fischman to date after she
was widowed. The chances of a woman remarrying after
age sixty were statistically inferior to the chances of an
associate in a law firm making partner. In both cases, you
sort of knew from the beginning who would make it.
There was a terrifying relentlessness in their eyes that set
them apart. Ida never had it. Not when it came to men or
money.

Nina was so terrifyingly unrelentless that she couldn't
even get married in the first place.

Yet there was Roz—cheating on her husband for years,
then sniffing around Peter Slater as soon as Andy died. All
this at an age when hot flashes were imminent, if not

already arriving. And at a weight that no one would admit to, much less flaunt. How did she pull it off?

The magazines never ran articles like "Old and Fat— How to Make it Work for You." But that was really what everyone wanted to know. A lot of black women knew how. She'd see them on the subway in their tank dresses with huge mounds of arms poking through, looking sexy as anything. While the white women, even those who were much less moundier, hid every extra ounce of flesh under layers and layers. Let's face it, Nina thought, if anyone is going to launch *FAT!* magazine, it's going to have to be an African American. Unless it's Roz.

"So," Nina said, "do you think that Roz's wide circuit had anything to do with Andy's death?"

"Not really. Roz probably married him for things that had nothing to do with sex. And he probably married her knowing all about her roving eye."

"Roving eye. What an old-fashioned expression."

"Okay, roving vagina. Is that better?" Ida asked.

"I like the sound of it."

"Why don't you talk to some of Andy's friends about Roz's roving vagina? Ask Ken. Maybe he has some ideas."

"I don't know," Nina said. "I guess I've been avoiding talking to him. But then, I always avoid talking to him."

"There are worse. Believe me. Rose Jaffee's son-in-law attends baseball camp every Passover. And he used his cellular phone in the middle of Rose's niece's wedding ceremony at the Pierre."

"Ma, I've met Rose Jaffee. She's lucky he lets her see her grandchildren. When they write the sequel to that book and call it *Toxic Grandparents* they should devote a whole chapter to Rose Jaffee."

"Yeah, maybe. But her son-in-law deserves her."

"What does he do?"

"He's a psychiatrist."

"Of course," Nina said. "What else would he be?"

"A lawyer?"

"Good one."

"Too obvious."

"Maybe. Anyway," Nina said, "I think I'll call Ken tomorrow and try to wedge myself into his busy but spectacular life."

"I'm telling you, he's a different person since he got a permanent parking spot."

"It's hard to imagine him generous of spirit," Nina said.

"Well, I don't know if I'd go that far. But he's generally in a much better mood. Call him. You'll see."

CHAPTER NINETEEN

NINA HAD TO MEET KEN at his office, in between patients. Which was fine with her, since the office was just a few blocks away on Central Park West. Besides, Nina was, at long last, in the position of having nothing better to do with her day than fit herself into other people's schedules.

The office was pleasant without being flashy. Every now and then Ken would have a famous client, but he wasn't the kind of dermatologist who fluttered around celebrities, trying to get under their skin and into their wallets. Or bedrooms. His patients expected him to be expensive without being ludicrous, to be quoted from time to time in an article in a reputable periodical, but not to have his own cable television show. And not to do drugs or have affairs.

Ken had never been the star-fucker type. It was Nina's private opinion that he was too self-absorbed to notice whether somebody else happened to be famous. In the family he had grown up in, the Rubins of Syosset, with two younger sisters and an adoring mother, Ken had been the star. And that notion remained permanently fixed in his mind. While he might take note from time to time how much wealth another person had accumulated, Ken continued to play center stage in his own mental firmament.

Because he wasn't a star-fucker, it was easier for him to

remain faithful to Laura. For one thing, she threw off some of the reflected light from Ken's stardom. Not as much as his children, but enough to elevate her in status. And his was a fixed universe; the heavenly bodies stayed where they were. It would be unseemly to throw a planet out of your solar system simply because she was getting varicose veins. And you certainly didn't take a younger, hotter one into your orbit. Not with your kids watching.

And so Ken was, for all intents and purposes, the perfect husband. Laura had always been a smart shopper. While Ida and Nina were still cruising the aisles of Alexander's, perplexedly staring at garments made for Puerto Rican teenagers, Laura was up the block at Loehmann's, shrewdly scooping up discounted items designed for the Upper East Side.

And she had shopped just as well for a college. On a limited budget, she had chosen the Cornell School of Human Ecology. It had the tuition of a state university, but proximity to the more expensive School of Liberal Arts. Nina, on the other hand, had spent her undergraduate years at the State University of New York at Stony Brook, in a tripled dorm room, surrounded by unlandscaped grounds and the children of postal workers.

Laura had never wanted to be around poor people. The Bronx was history, as far as she was concerned, and she had never really enjoyed any of her history classes. So when it came time to find a husband (the thought occurred to Laura several decades before it occurred to Nina) she cruised the premed department exclusively. And after only a few false starts, she came up with the perfect specimen.

Laura's perfect specimen sat behind a desk the size of a studio apartment. "To what do I owe this honor?" he asked.

"I wanted to ask you a few questions," Nina said. "About Roz and Andy."

"Okay." He glanced at his watch in one of those sneaky little gestures that allows both people to pretend the glance was going unnoticed.

The watch-peeking annoyed Nina, since she wouldn't have been running around like this to begin with if it hadn't been for her brother-in-law. Up until the evening that Laura had called her and begged her to investigate, she had happily been drifting through her life, wasting day after day, making up for lost time. Since Laura's call, she had actually been forced to take the D train deep into Brooklyn and now here she was, sitting and staring at a stack of pamphlets that described the treatment of rosacea.

"What's rosacea?" she asked.

"Why? What does rosacea have to do with Roz and Andy?"

"Nothing, I just wondered. You have that whole stack of pamphlets there and I never even heard of it." She knew she was wasting his time, paying him back for sneaking a look at his watch. But she didn't care.

"Yeah, all of a sudden everybody thinks they've got it. Nobody had ever even heard of it until Jane Brody wrote it up in the *Times*. I can't tell you how many calls I got the week that the article ran." He paused and leaned into Nina's face. "Actually, you might have a mild case."

"Me?"

"I think so. Does your face turn red when you drink alcohol or eat spicy foods?"

"Definitely. My nose gets so red when I drink that sometimes I look like W. C. Fields."

"He had it."

"W. C. Fields had rosacea?"

"Yup. Everyone thinks he looked that way because he

was an alcoholic. But it was actually an advanced case of rosacea, probably exacerbated by his drinking."

"Don't tell me I'm going to look like that one day." She had spent so much time worrying about ending up like Simone Signoret, it had never occurred to her that things could get even worse.

"It's treatable," Ken said. "We'll start you with a topical antibiotic."

"Are you sure it's rosacea?"

"Well, it definitely looks like that to me. Although the disease is more common in blond Celtic types than in Jewish people with brown hair."

Nina considered launching into an explanation of how she was really more of a blonde than a brunette and had only dyed her hair darker because of her great strength of character, that a weaker woman would have gone for the highlights. But she was used to losing Ken in the middle of her sentences and lately had been trying to avoid it before it happened.

"What causes it?" she asked.

"They think it's the result of millions of tiny mites living in your facial pores."

"Oh, there's a great image." Nina wasn't normally squeamish when it came to blood and guts, but microorganisms drove her totally crazy.

Ken scribbled something on a pad. "Here's a prescription for the cream. Twice a day, morning and night. It should clear up quickly. You've only got a mild case." He handed her the piece of paper. "Now, what else can I do for you?"

"Have you been questioned again by the police regarding Andy's murder?"

"No, just that one time."

"Well, Laura was quite upset when that happened. And she asked me to look into things. And I have."

Ken looked amused, if anything. "You collect murders the way some women collect husbands," he said.

"I hope it's not an either/or situation."

"What happened with your boyfriend, Jonathan?"

"It's over."

"I liked him," Ken said. "He was pretty normal."

"A refreshing change, huh?"

"Well, yeah." Ken picked at a nail. They weren't polished, but they were awfully clean.

"Perhaps normal boyfriends will be the beginning of a new trend."

"Maybe. I know an oncologist who's getting divorced," he said. "Gary Spitzer. I think you met him."

"Isn't he the one at that party you gave who named his daughter Demi?"

"That's right."

"Forget it."

"It was his wife's fault. She insisted on the name and he couldn't talk her out of it."

"Well, take it from me, anyone who married her wouldn't want to marry me."

"But he learned his lesson."

"I doubt it. Those kinds of mistakes are bred in the bone." She caught sight of her newly dark hair out of the corner of her eye. "Besides," she said, her voice half an octave lower, "I did not find Dr. Spitzer the least bit attractive. If I recall correctly, he was incapable of carrying on a normal conversation. He subjected a roomful of people to ten minutes of obsessing about his lease renewal negotiations."

"But Gary had an escalation clause that was a real ball buster."

"Who cares? Certainly no one in that room. Anyway, you've done enough for one day, diagnosing and treating my rosacea. You can't be expected to cure my marital condition. But I appreciate the attempt."

"Anytime."

"Okay. I might take you up on it. But let's get back to Andy. How did he die?"

"Poison is what I heard. One of his colleagues was telling me about it at the memorial service. I can't remember exactly what he said, but I think he said it was a substance that doesn't kick in for a day or so. Which means that they can't pinpoint where Andy was when he ingested it."

"Interesting. So anyone could be a suspect."

"Right." Ken looked at his watch again, this time more blatantly. "So since they can't narrow it down by opportunity, they are looking at motive. Which is why they came around to see me."

"You mean this business about the apartment house in Borough Park?"

"Yeah. It's so ridiculous—because Andy begged me to go into that deal with him. I mean really, who wants to own real estate? Especially a building full of old people in Brooklyn. But he needed me, so I agreed to it. I had a feeling it would end in a mess, but I never imagined this."

"So you and Andy always got along pretty well?" she asked. "No major blowups?"

"No fights at all. He was an incredibly easygoing guy. He got along with everybody. That's why I can't figure this thing out."

"What about his marriage? Not stormy? Because Roz seems like a difficult woman."

"Oh, she's impossible. But he always worshipped her, no matter how much of a pain in the ass she was. I was continually amazed. I'd sit there and watch one of her tantrums and was sure that the next day Andy would take the kids and flee the jurisdiction. But he hung in, taking an incredible amount of shit from her."

"Did he know that she was cheating on him?" Nina asked.

"I think she cut that out a long time ago."

"Before she had the children?"

"It must have been. Because I remember some story about her being pregnant or trying to get pregnant while she tested positive for chlamydia. I think that scare put an end to Roz's risky behavior."

"And she never resumed it?"

"As far as I know."

"Is there someone I could talk to who Andy was really close to?" Nina asked. "In whom he confided on a daily basis? Who would be more current than you?"

"Why don't you talk to that colleague of his that I met at the memorial service. He seemed to know a lot of what went on in Andy's life. While you're at it, check out the lab. It's an interesting place."

"What's this guy's name?"

"It's David something. Levinson, I think. Maybe Leventhal, I can't remember."

Nina pictured a guy in a maroon crew neck sweater eating caponata at the memorial service. "Is he the guy with glasses and curly hair?"

"Yeah, that's him. A lot of hair."

"I met him," Nina said. "Well, I didn't really meet him. But I did manage to listen to him for a while. Do you know how I could contact him?"

"If you call Andy's number at the lab, you'll still get his voice mail. I guess they never got around to erasing his message. But if you push zero, you'll get the receptionist. She should be able to find David whatever-his-name-is."

"That's fine."

This time it was Nina who looked at her watch in a grand gesture. And Ken said, almost deferentially, "Keep me posted on the rosacea."

CHAPTER
TWENTY

DAVID LEVENBERG was wearing the same sweater he had been wearing the last time Nina saw him. What kind of person, Nina wondered, would pick maroon over heathered purple and hunter-green and all the other evocative shades that Shetland wool crew necks were made in? Maroon evoked nothing other than memories of eighth grade, a particularly drab year for Nina. She had shunned the color ever since, refusing even to carry Macy's shopping bags until they changed the design.

Nina tried to give David the benefit of the doubt. Perhaps a parent had bought it for him, a particularly cautious mother who had been taught the importance of not letting your children stand out. Or maybe he had the kind of color blindness that makes everything look green except for shades of the maroon family. There was always the possibility that he wore it to conceal guinea pig bloodstains that occasionally soaked through his lab coat. More than likely, however, David Levenberg was just a maroon kind of guy.

Although the buildings at Morgan were grand, the lab didn't seem all that different from her high school biology laboratory. There were stainless steel counters and deep wide sinks and lots of test tubes, just the way she remembered. The major improvement seemed to be a communal coffeepot, which they hadn't had at Bronx

Science. He led Nina over to the coffee and poured her a cup. "Have a seat," he said.

She accepted. He joined her. "I hope I'm not disrupting your day," Nina said.

"I'm okay for about forty-five minutes. Then I have to go and check on something."

"I'll try to be brief. But it's not exactly what I'm best at." She waited for a laugh, but moved on when she realized that got no response. "As I mentioned on the phone," she continued, "I'm doing some research for an article that's going to run in *The New Yorker*."

She paused again to see if he had any sort of reaction. But he didn't give her the same sort of fluttery gush that most people did at a mention of the august publication. He just grunted a little impatiently and waited for her to continue. So she did. "There were some allegations about a cover-up in the Brooklyn D.A.'s office regarding Andy's murder. Although, so far, I haven't come up with any solid evidence."

"Oh, yeah," he said. "I talked to Roz about that. She exaggerates, you know."

It was a simple way of putting it, yet perfectly accurate. Nina supposed that was the point of scientists. David Levenberg was trained to report the empirical truth as he observed it. He would give you the same answer whether you had just charmed the pants off him or not. So why bother warming him up?

"You know how he was killed, don't you?" David asked.

"He was poisoned, wasn't he?"

"Right. I actually spoke with the coroner's office about the specifics."

"You did?" Nina asked. "How come?"

"Just curious."

She couldn't decide whether this came under the category of suspicious behavior or not. Nina thought of her friend's son who had insisted on turning his dead cat over with a spatula to inspect it more closely. "He's either going to be a surgeon or a homicidal maniac," the friend had said. "According to the Minnesota Multiphasic Personality Index, there's very little difference between the two. We're hoping for a surgeon, anyway."

David Levenberg probably was just curious, Nina decided. "What did the coroner say?" she asked.

"Apparently Andy ingested a toxic amount of methanol. Are you familiar with the substance?"

"No, I'm not."

"It's an alcohol compound, used in various common household products. Also in moonshine. The unusual thing about it is that it doesn't kill you right away. It doesn't even produce any side effects for at least twelve hours. Usually more."

"I think Roz told me that Andy was home when he died," Nina said. "Is that right?"

"Right. Home in bed. The time of death was between eight and nine in the morning."

"So where was he the day before?"

"Here, in the lab. Drinking coffee the entire day, I might add. As was his habit."

"From this very pot?" Nina couldn't stop herself from slamming her coffee cup down with a bit of alarm.

David smiled, but not without condescension. "No, they took that away for chemical analysis. Useless, really, since the pot had already been scrubbed clean at the end of the day."

"And Roz found him, didn't she?"

"Yeah, she told me that she let him sleep in because he had worked really late the night before. By the time she went to wake him up, he was already dead."

"So he probably ingested the methanol sometime during the previous day?" Nina asked.

"Probably."

It was hard to tell whether David Levenberg was hiding something or not. Nina was so used to lawyers, with their subtext and manipulation. Scientists were a breed apart. Or were they? She thought back to the kids she had gone to high school with, the ones in the advanced placement science courses who had grown up to wear lab coats.

Even if it was true that scientists spent a lot of time fighting over grants and tenure, Nina was sure that she remembered more duplicity among the students who had volunteered for political campaigns and had grown up to be attorneys and speechwriters. The AP chem class, although not particularly glamorous, had an innocence and earnestness about it. It wasn't the kind of place where you had to worry about being stabbed in the back or slipped methanol in your coffee. Not like in the poly-sci club, where everyone was always looking over your shoulder as if some movie star was suddenly going to walk into the room.

Nevertheless, in their own funny way, the science geniuses back at high school were the most glamorous of all the students. The truly brilliant ones had awesome reputations, and could do whatever they wanted, like a star quarterback on a Big Ten campus. They cut English to work in the lab and wore eyeglass frames that had gone out of style years before without sustaining the least bit of critical gossip. They got away without showers and haircuts for periods of time that would be unacceptable for anyone else. They didn't date, of course, but almost no one did. Sexual activity back then was like football—the Bronx High School of Science just didn't have a team.

Nina couldn't really tell whether David Levenberg was a science genius or just a guy making a living. His eyeglass frames were au courant, but that was easy these days. A simple wire frame had settled into popularity a while ago and now you could have new lenses put into the same frame every two years without looking outdated. True, the maroon was not good, but not awful enough to make him a genius. She was unable to detect any sexual sparks emanating from him, but these days that made him normal, not off the curve.

"So," Nina said, "it's my understanding that Andy was working on a herpes vaccine. Is that correct?"

"Yeah, he was part of our team. There were three of us working on herpes research. Now it's just me and Tina."

"Had the three of you all been working together for a very long time?"

"About five years. Andy was here before us, working on some other stuff. But then he started the vaccine project going and we came and joined him."

"And it's been one big happy family?" she prompted.

"Pretty much."

"Wasn't there a lot of competition?"

"For what?"

"You know, getting grants, getting published, that kind of stuff." Nina wished she could be more specific, but all of her knowledge came from movies she'd seen and books she'd read too long ago.

"When we published, we published as a team. And our grants were awarded jointly, to all three of us, which is unusual."

"What's going to happen now?"

"What do you mean?"

"Well, now that Andy's dead, are you and Tina going to split the grant money two ways instead of three?" she asked.

"No, we're going to have to bring someone in to replace Andy. There's too much work for just the two of us to handle. We'd be total prisoners in the lab."

"Have you chosen someone yet?"

"We've got a few candidates," David said. "It's a decision that has to be made carefully, since the work is so specialized. There aren't too many people with the necessary experience."

Even if they all were one big happy family, Nina thought, perhaps there was someone who would kill to get in on the action. "I imagine," she said, "that there are quite a few people vying for the position. After all, Morgan University is such a prestigious place."

"You'd be surprised how much recruiting we have to do."

"Really?"

"Yeah, it's not easy to get someone to give up a tenured position at a university in some pleasant, mid-size city to come to New York and be faced with the dilemma of where their family is going to live."

"I can see that." Out in California, she had been amazed to find that companies now had difficulty convincing prospective employees to pack up and move to Los Angeles. America had become a nation of people who all wanted to relocate to Fort Collins, Colorado.

"So we haven't hired anyone yet," David said. "And I don't know when we will. Meanwhile, Tina and I are working literally around the clock to keep on track."

"So who do you think killed Andy?" she asked. "Keeping in mind, of course, that he could easily have been poisoned right here in the lab."

"I really have no idea," he said.

She believed that David had no idea. For the same reason that she believed Jonathan when he told her that he had no idea whether the colleague he worked with for years was married. Or where his boss had grown up. Or whether the guy he played tennis with on Tuesdays was gay. Men were so useless sometimes.

"David, can you do me a favor?" she asked.

"What's that?"

"Could you see if Tina will speak with me?"

CHAPTER
TWENTY-ONE

DAVID WENT OFF to look for Tina and came back to report that she was in a meeting. She'd be available in half an hour, he said. Rather than make the effort of trying to engage David Levenberg in thirty more minutes of conversation, Nina opted to run over to First Avenue for coffee and a muffin. She loved muffins, but acknowledged them for the fraud that they were. After all, if it weren't for the word *muffin*, everyone would be eating cake for breakfast all week.

When Tina finally showed up, she was, as Nina expected, the Asian American woman in the red vest, the one who had been gently teasing David at Andy's memorial service. Today, in place of the red vest, she wore a long, loose dress in a sedate navy print. It was the kind of dress that Nina would have worn, but not if she weighed 110 pounds. Nina supposed that in cultures where thinness prevailed, as among Asians, you could be casual about it. But when thinness became a rare commodity, as among Jews, you had to dress for it. Actually, Nina noticed that since she had given up the thought of being blond, there had been a spillover effect on her weight. Not that she no longer thought about being thin at all, but she thought about it a lot less.

"Hi, I'm Tina Hsu." She introduced herself and extended her hand.

"Nina Fischman. Thanks for seeing me."

"So here we are. Tina and Nina."

"That's right. Hey, doesn't anybody wear labs coats around here?" Nina asked.

"Why, is this a photo op?"

"What do you mean?"

"Well, David told me that you're writing an article for *The New Yorker*. I thought maybe you needed a photograph."

Tina Hsu was going to be a lot more forthcoming than David Levenberg, Nina could tell that already. Of the two, the Jew was definitely the inscrutable one. For gossip, you'd have to go with gender over ethnicity. A lot of the time, girls did just want to have fun.

"No, no photograph," Nina said. "Actually, I'm just doing some research about Andy's murder. Trying to dig around and see whether there's a cover-up going on."

"That's not the kind of story that they usually cover, is it?"

"The magazine has gotten a lot more . . . um . . . tabloidy lately, if you know what I mean. But they still don't run too many photos, I don't think."

Tina led her over to a couple of upholstered chairs in an adjacent lounge area. "The only reason I asked," she said, "was because there's been so much press around this place lately. And they always seem to be taking the dopiest photographs you can imagine."

"Really? Press? How come?"

"You haven't been reading about the fat mouse gene by any chance, have you?"

"Are you kidding? Of course I have." Science had finally found out what women had known in their hearts all along. That you, along with some of the mice in the world, were fat not because you didn't hold the mayo or had opted out of the triathlon circuit. But because some little piece of one of your chromosomes had determined that you were going to have to spend the rest of your life in tasteful but loose-fitting clothing and that there was never going to be any point in attending a sample sale no matter how hard you tried.

"Well," said Tina, "most of the research on the fat mice was done right here. And whenever they have the tiniest breakthrough, they send out all these press releases. And then we get so many reporters and photographers you'd think we'd discovered the cure for cancer."

"I think there are a lot of people who would rather have cancer than be fat," Nina said.

"I know. Jesus, obesity isn't even a terminal illness."

"It's not?" The word had such chilling connotations, it seemed worse than terminal.

"No. Obesity is often found in attendance with other diseases, but it's the diabetes or hypertension that will kill you, not the obesity. There are plenty of fat people who live well into their nineties."

"Like my grandmother," Nina said. "Come to think of it, my mother's always been pretty fat, and she's one of the healthiest seventy-five-year-olds I know."

"See? It's a myth. Americans are so terrified of being fat, they'll do anything to prevent it. And that's why Elliott is going to be retired on a hundred-foot sailboat soon, while I'm going to be sitting in this lab forever, studying the lesions on guinea pig labia."

"Who's Elliott?"

"He's our resident celebrity, the guy who's heading up the obesity research. They're just about to announce that they've successfully replicated leptin. And as soon as they get it on the market, I guarantee you, Elliott will be out of here so fast, my papers will fly in the breeze."

"And leptin has something to do with fat mice?" Nina asked.

"It's the substance that's produced by the gene that controls obesity. If the leptin's off, the mouse is rotund. But all you have to do is shoot him up with a little extra leptin and he becomes a furry little bathing beauty in nothing flat."

"And I assume that Elliott is busy trying to synthesize leptin for human use?"

"It's only a matter of time. And not much time. Apparently the models for the mice and human blood chemistry are pretty much identical."

"My God," Nina said. "No more fat people in the world. I find it hard to imagine."

"Elliott always tells the press that the injections will only be available for the morbidly obese. But I'd be surprised if that's the way it plays out."

"Yeah, that sounds like a total crock. I'm sure that any rich lady who's obsessed enough is going to get her hands on the stuff, don't you think?"

"Absolutely."

"Well, I'm not going to invest in any fat farms from now on, I'll tell you that."

Tina sat back and crossed her legs. "And to think," she said, "all this could have been Andy's."

"What do you mean?"

"Andy used to work with Elliott."

"When?"

"Back in the fatty Zucker days."

"Fatty Zucker? Like Fatty Arbuckle?"

"No, fatty Zuckers were a breed of fat rats that had been bred by some scientist named Zucker. Decades ago. Nina, you probably don't realize how long ago researchers determined obesity to be genetic."

"I guess I don't." *If I did,* she thought, *I wouldn't have spent the spring of 1989 eating nothing but powder.*

"But no one knew what to do about it. And then Andy

and Elliott isolated the gene that proved to be responsible. It was very exciting. Everyone was shocked when they split up and Andy completely changed tracks."

"And switched to herpes?"

"Yup."

"But that doesn't make sense," Nina said. "I don't mean to belittle the importance of your research. But why put years of your life into one field of research, finally have a big breakthrough, and then walk away from it?"

"Well, I wasn't here then. I joined Andy after he had already started up the herpes project. But I can see why he might have wanted to skip out on leptin. Not to mention Elliott."

"Why?"

"First of all, Elliott seems to have spent more of the past five years talking to pharmaceutical companies than doing any research. And Andy was a true scientist. He hated luncheon seminars and corporate P.R. people and all that bullshit. He just wanted to be in the lab."

"And Elliott?"

"He's the opposite."

"How did I guess?"

"Have you met him?"

"No, but I can imagine."

"Second of all, leptin made Andy nervous."

"In what way?"

"He couldn't stand all the ethical quandaries that scientists find themselves in these days. He was trained in the old school. You know, you pick a disease and try to find a cure for it. He didn't enjoy indulging in discussions of who has rights to frozen zygotes and that kind of thing."

"A lot of people find that stuff fascinating," Nina said.

"Not Andy. So whenever he had to examine the societal implications of making leptin available to the general public, he'd squirm. Even when he wasn't working on it anymore."

"So you think that was sufficient to make him drop his research and switch to something entirely different? Even though leptin is so potentially lucrative?" Nina wasn't buying it. Not with a wife who made hats and had expensive tastes in furniture and cocktail forks.

"And there was Elliott's personality," Tina said.

"What's he like?"

"You'll have to meet him."

"Okay, I will. But what about these animal rights people? Roz thinks that they're responsible for Andy's death. She claimed that they were always making threats against the people in the lab and that the Brooklyn D.A. is covering it up because his wife is somehow involved."

"Oh, that." Tina waved her hand dismissively.

"I asked David about it, but he just said that Roz exaggerates."

"Yeah, I wouldn't take any of those animal people too seriously. I remember Andy saying that he wasn't going to mention anything to her anymore because she always got all hysterical and upset the children."

"So it was much ado about nothing?"

"Yeah, just a couple of old ladies that live in the neighborhood gave out leaflets once with pictures of albino hamsters. It was just silliness."

"What about the graffiti?"

"Graffiti? Oh, yeah, years ago somebody got in and spray-painted some slogans in the lab. It never happened again."

"So you always felt safe coming here at night?"

"Nina, I grew up downtown, where every teenage boy, whether he was Spanish or Chinese, had to be in a gang just to protect himself. Am I going to be afraid of a couple of society matrons on York Avenue? Please."

"So what do you think happened to Andy?"

"I don't know." Tina distraughtly pulled her hair back into a tight ponytail and held it there for a minute. "At first I thought it was an accident. That's what we all wanted to believe. But it couldn't have been, could it?"

"It doesn't sound like it."

"Well, it wasn't David or myself. If that's what you're thinking. The three of us worked superbly together and we miss him terribly. We were far better off with Andy than without him."

"I believe you," Nina said. And she did.

"I'm sorry." Tina got up and moved toward the door. "If I think of anything else . . ."

"You've been very generous with your time," Nina said. "I appreciate it."

"Oh, please. Anytime."

"Um, Tina, one more thing. Do you think . . . ?" Nina's voice trailed off.

"What?"

"Oh, never mind."

"No, tell me."

"I know this probably sounds really silly to you, but do you know if Elliott is looking for volunteers for any of his experiments?"

"I think they're still using mice in their trials. But even when they get up to humans, they're probably going to be looking for really fat people. You know, morbidly obese."

"Of course. Forget I said anything."

"I will."

Nina blushed for a good while.

CHAPTER
TWENTY-TWO

"THAT'S RIDICULOUS," Ida said.

"What's ridiculous?" Her mother's statement made her mentally run through everything that was ridiculous. And at the top of the list was Nina's life.

"Why would Andy Campbell drop out of the highest-profile and most potentially lucrative medical research going on in the entire country? It doesn't make sense."

Nina and Ida were taking a walk. It was one of those unusually mild December days that send New Yorkers scurrying out-of-doors in a desperate last attempt to fend off Seasonal Affective Disorder. Nina was enjoying their stroll, but had to admit that she felt somehow retarded, tagging after her mother down Riverside Drive even though she had passed the age of forty.

The awful secret that kept gnawing at Nina, the one that she hadn't told anybody, was how pleasant her meaningless existence was. How much easier it was to not have to make a living, to sponge off of someone. Except for those few hot, depressed, surreal months in Los Angeles with Jonathan, she had never before been able to experience the art of being a parasite.

There was a soothing quality to not getting any bills or magazines or even any mail addressed to Occupant. Because technically Nina didn't qualify as an occupant anymore. She still took up space, but she didn't occupy any.

Even her sexless existence was soothing in a way. There was no anxiety about whether to have sex or whether it was going to be any good. And aside from several nightmares that could easily be attributable to severe sexual frustration, Nina found celibacy to be surprisingly relaxing.

She could probably go on like this forever—reading the *Times*, doing the crossword puzzle, drinking coffee, doing an exercise video, seeing the two o'clock show at the Lincoln Plaza Cinema, ordering out Chinese food and compulsively reading fiction until midnight. And then sleeping late in her twin bed and doing the same thing all over again the next day. With an occasional foray into investigating Andy's murder. What it amounted to was being a schnorrer and Nina was loving every minute of it.

Well, almost every minute. Because there were, of course, those occasions when the angel of anxiety would visit down upon her and thunder into her ear various warnings about doing something with the rest of her life. And there were also times when her mother would come into her room at ten A.M. and gaze upon the not-quite-awake Nina with a worried eye and mutter something about how life was not supposed to be a continual replay of Christmas break during your sophomore year of college.

So when Ida said "That's ridiculous," even though they were in the middle of a conversation about Andy Campbell, Nina took it a little personally. So she was relieved when it turned out that her mother was talking about his abortive departure from the leptin lab. "Who is this Elliott guy?" Ida asked.

"I don't even know his last name," Nina said.

"Find out. And then go see him. There's something screwy going on here. I don't see why Andy would give up on something so big."

"Well, Andy didn't seem like an especially shrewd businessman. He probably cared more about science than money."

"Even if he did have a *goyisheh kop*," Ida said, "his wife certainly doesn't. Besides, if he cared so little for money, why did he own half of an apartment building in Borough Park? For creative fulfillment?"

"I explained that to you. He did it as a favor to his father-in-law."

"I never had the pleasure of meeting Mr. Brillstein. But I'll bet he wasn't the kind of guy who would hand an investment like that over to someone who was a complete idiot about money. Andy must have had something on the ball."

"Maybe," Nina suggested, "he thought that a drug with the potential to stamp out fat people was politically incorrect. And he didn't want to be responsible for their obliteration." She knew she didn't sound convincing. In Nina's experience, male Christian ectomorphs were the last people on earth that wondered what made fat people tick. Men like Andy always figured that if you trained hard enough, anyone could get down to a six-minute mile. But then again, he was married to Roz Brillstein.

"Talk to Roz," Ida said, as if reading her daughter's mind. "Even before you talk to Elliott."

"I don't know how much Andy told her about what went on in the lab. After all, she didn't know about his ownership in the apartment building."

"It might be interesting," Ida said, "to hear what Roz has to say about fat mice."

"I'm sure it will. And what do you have to say about fat mice, Ma?"

Ida paused a moment. "You first," she finally said.

"Okay, here goes. I would like to be politically correct on the subject. To be able to say that the human race was created in diversity, that people are all shaped differently the same way that some dogs are dachshunds and some are Afghan hounds. And that my body serves me well. I would like to be grateful that my fat deposits are strategically placed low down so that I can sit for long periods of time and that my fat cells are far enough away from my heart to avoid the threat of cardiac disease. And also to be glad that they're plentiful enough to help me survive a winter famine should I suddenly be transported back to an Eastern European shtetl. And to thank God that I have enough body fat to keep my estrogen supply elevated to the point that should I ever choose to procreate, I would have an easier time than someone with no fat reserves. I know I should feel lucky. My body's never given me a moment of trouble because of its size, except for the fact that I sometimes have to apply powder between my thighs in July.

"I understand all this," Nina continued. "But where do I fall on a one-to-ten scale of self-acceptance? I would be embarrassed to say."

"So you'd go for the leptin?" Ida asked.

"In a minute. How about you?"

"The great thing about getting old is that it's easy to be a revolutionary. There's nobody there to fire me or divorce me because of what I say or how I look. I've also gotten to the point where I'm more worried about my body falling apart than I am about making it get any smaller. I'm glad it's all in one piece, no matter what size it is."

"So this all seems like trivial nonsense to you?"

"Let me finish. What I was going to add is that I'm more scarred than you are. I've lived almost twice as long, been on twice as many diets, failed twice as many times, looked at twice as many magazines with twice as many skinny models. You can't walk away from all that so easily."

"I guess not," Nina said.

"In addition, I didn't grow up in a period of affluence like you did, with everyone on campus letting it all hang out. I came of age in the Depression, when everyone was too nervous not to conform."

"How can you say that? The thirties were a time when the American left was at its height."

"Oh, please, don't talk to me about the American left." Ida rolled her eyes. "The only way most of us could get up the nerve to rebel against our parents was to join the Communist Party. Which turned out to be an organization with so many rules and hierarchies that it made both the FBI and Orthodox Judaism look like . . . um . . . um . . ." She groped for an analogy.

"A Grateful Dead road tour?" Nina suggested.

"I guess so. Anyway, my generation was a very scared one. We were scared of failing to assimilate, scared of going broke, scared of Hitler and then, later, scared of Joseph McCarthy. It stands to reason all of the women were scared of being fat. And I'm not claiming to be immune."

"But, Ma, if fat phobia is a children-of-immigrants kind of thing, what accounts for the fact that it only seems to be getting worse? That skinny fourteen-year-old WASPs are going into their private school bathrooms and sticking their fingers down their throats?"

"I don't know." Ida led them over to a bench next to the Sailors' and Soldiers' Monument near Eighty-ninth Street. They sat and looked at New Jersey for a few moments. Out there was America, a nation of women who seemed as tortured as ever. A few years from now, when leptin prescriptions would undoubtedly be written with reckless abandon, would they be any happier?

Nina took a quick assessment of her life, measuring it against Ida's. Here she was at the end of the century, an unemployed spinster living with her mother. Did she feel pathetic? Well, she felt frustrated, ambivalent, periodically depressed, and incurably neurotic. But not pathetic.

She also did not feel beside the point, the way she probably would have felt had she found herself in the same circumstances at the middle of the century. Well, that was measurable progress, she supposed. And she had done it all without the benefit of leptin.

"So what are you going to do next?" asked Ida.

"Talk to Roz, I guess."

"I meant in a more general way."

"Stay in New York. Look for a job. Then get an apartment. Go back to being Nina Fischman."

"Not such a terrible thing, is it?"

"No, I guess not," Nina said. "Besides, it's the only game in town."

CHAPTER
TWENTY-THREE

WHEN NINA CALLED ROZ, she made her same noises about her schedule and her hats and her shrink and her kids. So Nina, in her new brunette voice, suggested that she was willing to jump on a train to Brooklyn that very minute and come straight over to Roz's house. There was really no way for Roz to wriggle out of it, so she politely assented.

Nina's subway ride was uneventful except for a conductor who kept announcing all the stations as if they were major tourist attractions. The riders, with their glazed eyes and crumpled tabloids, ignored him.

Roz opened the door, dressed in a "Moonlight in Morocco" theme with embroidered carpet slippers and a floor-length djellaba with a swatch of kilim fabric stitched across the shoulders. Nina glanced around the room to see where Roz had dropped her fez, but the only visible headgear was a horned Valhalla helmet set on a shelf next to some pre-Columbian figures.

"I have mint tea already made," Roz offered.

"I'll bet you do," Nina said.

"Would you like some?"

"Sure."

Roz brought out the tea in what was probably an authentic North African teapot with matching cups, but their ceramic pedigree eluded Nina, who had limited porcelain expertise.

"Where are the kids?" Nina asked. She was curious to see if Roz dressed them to match her theme du jour. Perhaps they were sitting in the kitchen wearing miniature fezzes and smoking a little hookah.

"They're upstairs, hopefully doing their homework, but probably watching television." It was odd to see this exotic creature in a djellaba playing the exasperated mom, but Roz seemed genuinely concerned.

"Well, I wanted to talk to you about Andy's work in the lab," Nina said.

"It's funny. That's the only thing I don't miss about him. All that endless obsessing about guinea pig lesions. It was all so boring."

Nina had always felt that science was exalted far above law—insofar as it was an empirical search for the truth, while law was more along the lines of shoddy hucksterism for whoever would pay you a quick buck. But there was no doubt in Nina's mind that they were both boring.

"Yeah, I'm sure it could get boring," she said to Roz. "The one thing I couldn't figure out after I talked to Tina and David was why Andy stopped doing leptin research. Especially just when he was about to have a breakthrough."

"Mmmm." Roz let out a long sigh and sipped her tea. "Well, it's really water under the bridge. I try not to think about it, but I guess it doesn't matter now."

"What doesn't matter?"

"My history. My ancient history with Elliott."

"Oh." Nina turned her attention to her teacup. She was afraid to look Roz straight in the eye for fear Roz would clam up. If Nina pretended that Roz wasn't there, perhaps she'd be more forthcoming. Nina sampled her mint tea. Mint was only one of the flavors that was identifiable in the intricate blend. There were layers upon layers of different tastes. Like Roz herself, who apparently somewhere beneath the surface harbored a layer of ancient history with Elliott.

"Actually," Roz said, "it had been over for years by the time Andy found out. That was the stupid thing about the whole goddamn affair."

"Affair?"

"I wouldn't call it an affair. The word connotes sneaking off to hotel rooms and doing other things that show up on the American Express bill, like sending flowers and buying lingerie. Elliott and I didn't carry on anything like that. We had a simple one-night stand and left no receipts."

"How did it happen?"

"Oh, it was so long ago. I had just gotten married. I'm sure that I wasn't even pregnant yet. And Elliott was between wives. For a change."

"How many has he had?"

"Three so far. But I'd bet on at least four by the time it's all over. He's one of those horribly old-fashioned belt-notching types."

"Has belt-notching gone out of fashion?" Nina asked.

"Don't you think so? The combination of changing market conditions and the sexual revolution has made womanizing seem so beside the point. I mean, of course a guy can get laid. What's the big deal?"

"I guess you're right. It's like women who proudly tell you that they bought their dress on sale. Well, of course they did. Who buys anything retail anymore?"

"Right. Anyway," Roz continued, "as I said, Elliott was between wives. And Andy was out of town. His mother was in the midst of a breast cancer scare, so he went home to spend some time with her."

"Was he a good son?" It suddenly occurred to Nina

that she should go talk to the Campbells, but she found the thought of traveling to upstate New York in the middle of December to be extremely enervating.

"Yeah, he was pretty dutiful. Except for marrying me, of course."

"So Andy was out of town and . . . ?" Nina prompted.

"He was up at his parents' place and I was newly married and hadn't gotten used to this monogamy thing yet. I ran into Elliott in the Village, on my way home from my shrink."

"The same shrink you have now?"

"Yes. I'm going for a world record," Roz said.

"Don't forget, you'll have to beat my mother."

"Right. Anyway, Elliott and I had coincidentally both stopped at a magazine stand near Sheridan Square. The next thing I knew I was drinking wine in his sunken living room on Barrow Street and listening to Mose Allison records."

"I've always tried to watch out for white men who have extensive jazz collections," Nina said.

"Why?"

"I don't know, I find them dangerous. So anyway, it was just that once?"

"Have you met him?"

"No, not yet."

"When you do," Roz said, "you'll see why it was just that once. Elliott is an impulse buy, the kind of commodity that you realize is a mistake as soon as you bring it home. I should probably have left before the album was over, but you know how it is. An object in motion tends to remain in motion."

"And he never pursued you for a rerun?"

"Nah. Since he had already notched his belt, there was no point in bothering."

"So how did Andy find out?"

"I still don't know. Obviously someone at the lab told him, but I never found out who or why."

"Andy wouldn't tell you?"

"Quite frankly, I was trying to minimize the whole thing. So there seemed no point in cross-examining him."

"But he did confront you?"

"Well, it all happened sort of backward." Roz refilled her cup. "First Andy told me that he wasn't going to be working with Elliott anymore. That he was dropping the obesity research and starting something else entirely different. Then, only after I pushed him did he admit to me that he had found out about my thing with Elliott. As a matter of fact, it turned out that he had known about it for a year before he said anything. He tried to stay on the project with Elliott, but ultimately decided that he just couldn't trust him anymore."

"But that he could still trust you?" It was out of Nina's mouth before she could stop herself.

Roz seemed unfazed by the question. "He loved me," she said simply. "He didn't love Elliott. Elliott was easier to leave."

"Did you try to talk him out of it?"

"At first. Not because I particularly cared for the partnership. By that time I knew Elliott was a back-stabbing, belt-notching jerk. And a lousy lay. But I felt that Andy's decision to make such a dramatic career move maximized what should have been a very minimal incident."

"What about the fact that your husband was willing to throw all of his research out the window before his big payoff? Certainly that must have mattered to you."

"Well, it did and it didn't." Roz crossed a leg and dangled a carpet slipper from her big toe.

"What do you mean?"

"I felt bad about Andy leaving before his big break.

Partly because of the money, I'll admit. But also because I knew what a brilliant and dedicated scientist he was and he deserved at least his fifteen minutes of fame."

Nina tried to imagine speaking these words about any male *Homo sapiens* of her acquaintance. She could not, however. "So that mattered to you. But you also said in some way it didn't matter."

"Well, there were two things. First of all, I was glad to get Elliott out of my life. Even though I was never the least bit tempted to replay the Barrow Street scene, he always made me uncomfortable. He'd give me this knowing little lecherous leer whenever we made eye contact. It made me want to kick him in the shins."

"And what else?"

Roz narrowed her eyes and ran her tongue over her teeth in thought. "I hated the whole idea of it," she finally said.

"Of what?"

"Of wiping out fat people."

"They weren't going to be wiped out, were they? Just made thin. That doesn't really count as genocide, does it?" Nina asked.

"What do you think of a belief system in which everyone is transformed into some kind of skinny *Übermensch*? In which diversity is eliminated? What does that remind you of, huh?"

"Um, I guess—"

"The next thing you know, the medical establishment is moving on to in utero genetic testing so that they can terminate pregnancies which would result in babies at the higher end of the weight curve."

"I see what you mean." Nina felt a few tears forming behind her eyelids.

"You're not skinny," Roz snapped. "You were probably never skinny."

"How'd you guess?"

"Do you consider yourself to have a birth defect?"

"No." Nina wished she sounded more convincing.

"I don't think that modern science necessarily agrees with you. If this thing is allowed to proceed to its natural conclusion, people will be aborting fetuses like you and only allowing people like your sister to be born."

That hit home. "A world full of Lauras. Gee."

"A sobering thought," Roz said.

"It's funny, because I always had the feeling that my mother considered Laura the mutant and me the true genetic heir. Laura's so . . . I don't know . . ."

"Thin."

"Right. But I have to admit, if I could trade bodies with my sister, I would."

"How come?" Roz challenged her.

"My life would be better."

"In what way?"

"I would have gotten married to a Jewish dermatologist in my early twenties?" Nina ventured.

"Oh, please." Roz flicked her hair back with her hand. Nina noticed a carved ivory bracelet with a Bakelite clasp. It went well with her forks. "You buy that crap about thin women having more sex appeal?"

"I think they play to a wider audience," Nina said. "At least in this culture."

"I never found that to be the case."

"But Roz, you're not normal. You're off the bell curve. As the statisticians say, you're an outlier."

"In what way?"

"I don't know, you must emit some pheromones that have men crawling all over you all the time."

"It's just a matter of attitude."

"I don't believe that," Nina said. "That's like telling some ghetto kid that anybody can get into Harvard, all they have to do is try. I think you have to be some kind of genetic mutant to grow up on welfare and end up at Harvard. It doesn't happen just because you're a good girl and do your homework. And it's just as much of a fraud to tell some poor little fat girl that if she gets a good haircut and wears small floral prints she'll get a date to the senior prom."

Roz said something in Yiddish that Nina didn't understand.

"Excuse me?" Nina asked.

"My mother was very fat when I was little. All the mothers were, even after we came to America. The women just couldn't stop eating after they got out of the camps. And my parents were delighted by how chubby I was. You know what they would do on their day off from the shop? They'd sew me outfits, then they'd dress me up in them and pinch my fat little arms. They were so happy."

Nina thought back. She supposed that Ida and Leo had pinched her fat little arms too. But she remembered them having a distinctly worried look while they were pinching.

"As far as I'm concerned," Roz said, "Elliott Adler is one step away from Joseph Mengele."

Now Nina knew his last name.

"It was the ones who lost weight easily that died in the camps, you know."

"I guess it was the one time when nobody would have wanted to be Audrey Hepburn or Jackie Kennedy," Nina said. "You didn't see too many people ordering carrot sticks and cigarettes for lunch after the war, huh?"

"Eating isn't a sin, you know," Roz said. "Or a sign of weakness. Appetite is a survival instinct. I just hope it doesn't take another Holocaust to make people in this country realize that."

"It will at least take a miracle. From what I can see, it's only getting worse."

"Well, soon it will be moot," Roz said. "Everyone will be getting their leptin injections and Elliott Adler will be one of the richest men in the world. He'll probably be up to wife number seven."

"And Roz Brillstein?"

"I'll still be sitting here in Park Slope, schlepping my hundred-and-sixty-seven-pound body around. But I can tell you one thing. I won't be sleeping alone."

"I believe you," Nina said.

"So go talk to Dr. Adler. See what he has to say. But don't forget what I told you."

"What's that?"

"He's a lousy lay."

CHAPTER
TWENTY-FOUR

ELLIOTT ADLER LOOKED less like a research scientist than almost anyone else Nina could think of. He had a slickness that she could picture on a half-hour infomercial selling . . . well, maybe selling leptin. He wore a ventless suit instead of a lab coat and his tie could easily have been from Hermès. His nails were not exactly polished, but definitely buffed or something. When he took Nina's hand, he gave it a firm squeeze, the kind of handshake that belonged in some marketing department somewhere. Elliott seemed quite ready to become rich and famous.

"So how long have you been writing for *The New Yorker?*" he asked.

He was the kind of guy who would not appreciate her downplaying her already paltry credentials. She'd lose his attention that way for sure. If she was smart, she'd tell him she had a film deal. "I've been working for them awhile," she said. "I mostly cover the local political scene. Originally there were some allegations about the Brooklyn D.A.'s office covering up certain aspects of the investigation of Andy's murder. That's how I got started on this story."

"I thought you told me that you were writing an article about the country's top ten medical researchers." His eyes blazed with indignation. That was the beautiful thing about true narcissists. They were thoroughly shameless.

"I said I was going to *propose* such an article to the magazine. But I need to do some more research before I can pitch them on it. And I'm just about finished with the story I'm working on. But I needed a few more details that I thought only you could supply."

"I see." He didn't sound the least bit mollified.

"So our meeting this morning is really killing two birds with one stone," she said. "You verify a few facts about Andy Campbell for me, and I can get enough information for a biographical sketch of you." Nina hoped that he believed her. She wasn't used to lying outside of court.

"Well, what do you need to know?" Now he sounded like he was going to rush off. She had to think of a way to reel him back in. Maybe if she started off with the biographical angle, she could warm him up so that he'd be more forthcoming when she asked him about Andy.

"I'm really more interested in you than Andy," she said. "Why don't you tell me about your childhood and education. We can start with that."

"Aren't you going to take notes?" he asked. Elliott had clearly been interviewed before.

"Not the first time around," Nina said, hoping she would get away with it. "I like to get a general idea of the person, then come up with a detailed set of questions afterward. At that point, I bring my tape recorder." She rummaged around her brain, trying to think of someone she could borrow one from, if it came to that. Her brother-in-law probably had one. He browsed in electronics shops the way Nina did in bookstores.

"Oh, okay." He sounded like he bought it. Elliott apparently liked the idea of an electronic device. He undoubtedly had a whole collection of expensive tape recorders tucked away in some wall unit somewhere.

"So did you grow up in New York City?" she asked.

"No. Allentown, Pennsylvania. My parents owned a dry goods store." He continued with a story that Nina had heard from so many out-of-town Jews. The small haberdashery becomes a department store. And the apartment over the dry goods shop becomes a sprawling suburban split-level. As one of the few Jews in school, the kid scoops up all the academic awards, shoves off for the Ivy League, and never looks back. Meanwhile, all the Jews that Nina grew up with in the Bronx had fathers who worked for the post office and mothers who insisted that their children stay home and commute to City College.

"I considered becoming a classics scholar," Elliott said, "but science proved to have an irresistible draw. So I went to medical school, where my Latin actually came in somewhat handy. Never did anything with all that Greek, however."

Nina supposed that a facility with dead languages could help get a guy laid. But when all is said and done, somebody is going to have to pick up the dinner tab. And the guy in the tweed jacket with the suede elbow patches probably is not carrying a gold card in his wallet.

"I didn't set out to be a researcher," he said. "I originally intended to become a clinician."

Probably a gynecologist, thought Nina.

"I enjoy dealing with people. And I think I'm quite good at it."

Who doesn't? she wondered. Sean Penn probably thinks he's good with people. Nina would bet her entire earring collection that Elliott was a lousy listener.

"But something drew me into obesity research," he continued. "Perhaps it was because of my family history. My maternal grandmother struggled with obesity her entire life."

"What a coincidence."

"Pardon?"

"All I mean is that almost every Jewish grandmother I've ever met was fat. I guess if you hang out with Yemenites, you'll see some thin ones. But otherwise . . ."

"Well, things don't have to be that way anymore," he said.

"Yes, tell me about your research. How you started and when you met Andy."

"We did a post-doc together."

"Here?"

"Yes, right in this lab. We never left. After all, where are you going to go when you leave Morgan? It's a place that you work hard to get to, not to leave."

"I can imagine."

"Besides, it's a one-way ticket that you can only use once. You know what I mean?"

"I think so."

"In other words, you're coming from Morgan, so you better go someplace good. Because if you don't, the next time you try to move, you'll be coming from someplace second-rate. And the fact that you used to be at Morgan might not be enough to help you out."

"So you're saying that people look mostly at the top of your résumé. So it pays to keep Morgan right up there."

"It's not only that, of course." Elliott took on a serious, professorial air. If he had a pipe, he would have chosen this moment to light it. "I care deeply about my work here. And I know that I can get the support I need here. The atmosphere is one where my work can thrive and there's no point in throwing that overboard, no matter how much money you're offered."

"Besides," Nina said, "I assume that money won't be an issue in the near future."

"Excuse me?"

"Once leptin gets on the market."

"Money always matters," he said. "Tell me, have you ever heard anyone speak the words *the money isn't an issue* and actually mean them?"

"Once. But I was out-of-town at the time."

"Anyway, neither Andy nor I ever really considered leaving Morgan. We were treated well here. And the research we were doing was very exciting. With a lot of potential." Elliott used the word *potential* the way someone selling limited partnerships in a real estate venture might use it.

"So were you working on obesity research from the beginning?" Nina asked.

"Almost. We fooled around on a few other things for a while, chased some wild gooses, hit some dead ends. But things really clicked when we zeroed in on the hypothalamus." He was practically licking his chops. And a fine set of chops they were—straight, evenly spaced teeth that spoke of expensive bridgework and bimonthly cleanings. A generous mouth with full lips that were frozen into a permanent public relations smile. A closely trimmed beard that made a statement of academia without nerdiness.

Nina tried to picture Elliott and Roz together, ten years ago, seducing each other over a bottle of chardonnay. The image got knocked off the screen, however, by Nina's memories of her own activities during that period.

Would she ever be on that treadmill again? Meeting, seducing, then call-waiting? She had been expecting the urge to kick in, but so far she was content to stay snugly wrapped in the fuzzy flannel cocoon of celibacy. The other night, a particularly chilly one, she had gone so far as to consider buying a pair of pajamas with feet.

Nina let her muscles relax to see if she could get any kind of sexual buzz from Elliott Adler, notorious beltnotcher and wife-snatcher. But all she felt was a detached, clinical admiration for his teeth. She had no more desire to stick her tongue between them than she had to eat black jelly beans, the ones she always left in the bottom of the jar.

Nina tore her eyes away from his teeth and reestablished eye contact. "At what point did you discover leptin?"

"Let's see. Andy and I had been working together for about five years when we finally came up with the early model for what would later become leptin. Of course, it took us a while longer to refine it."

"So why did he throw it all away?" she asked. "All those years of work? And so close to success."

"He must have been crazy." Elliott switched the high beams on for his dazzling P.R. smile.

"Was he? Crazy?"

"He was very intense. People like that are crazy some of the time. I used to tell him to calm down. After all, all we're really doing here is making a living. But I guess Andy didn't feel that way."

"What way did he feel?"

"Well, he wasn't the kind of guy you could just pick up and put down in another job. I couldn't picture him as a high school teacher or a periodontist."

"How about a dermatologist?" Elliott was less sincere than Ken, more manipulative. But Nina was sure that he would have made a tremendously successful dermatologist.

"No," Elliott said. "Andy could only have been what he was. A mad scientist." He gave a mean little "heh, heh" laden with contempt.

"So why did the two of you split up after all? Besides his being crazy."

"I don't know. He developed this obsession with the

herpes vaccine. Tina and David were working on it and he just used to drift over there, spending more time with them than on his experiments."

"Was there something strange going on? Was he having an affair with Tina, perhaps?" It didn't seem likely, Nina thought, but one never knew.

"Oh, no, I'm sure that wasn't the case. But sometimes I thought . . ."

"What?"

"Oh, I don't know if it's true or not. But it was my private theory that Andy must have had the disease himself. Otherwise why the obsession?"

"He never discussed it?"

"He denied it," Elliott said. "But I wouldn't have been surprised if he had the infection. His wife got around quite a bit, from what I understood."

"She told me she only slept with you once." There, that should shut him up. Nina had to remind herself that the point of an interview was not to shut the other person up. But it was too late to take back the words.

"And what does that have to do with your article for *The New Yorker*?" His P.R. smile had been transformed into a vicious leer. Roz's advice had been unnecessary. Nina had no need to keep her legs together because it was clear that Elliott Adler hated her guts. It was time to leave.

CHAPTER
TWENTY-FIVE

"A SCARY GUY."

"Well, then, it's no wonder Andy didn't want to keep on working with him," Ida said. "He sounds like a *putz*."

"But to give up all that research. A person doesn't throw out years of work just because his partner is a *putz*. Things don't work that way."

"Excuse me, but what way do they work?"

Ida and Nina were in the kitchen cooking, a less than annual event. But the barrage of seasonal images—plum pudding, gingerbread houses, and fragrant fruitcake—had finally gotten to the Fischman women.

Too traditional to indulge in blatant Christian baking, yet too lazy to make potato latkes, they had settled on kourabiedes, a type of butter cookie native to Greece. The fact that the recipe was of the Levantine, where it didn't snow at Christmas, somehow made their holiday culinary activities seem less *trayf*.

Baking was done in the Fischman household with even less frequency than other methods of cooking. Baking required a chemical precision that eluded Nina and Ida, both of whom considered measuring ingredients into eighths of a teaspoon to be the functional equivalent of exhibiting a neat Catholic school handwriting. A lifetime of disappointments had resulted—oozy cookie batters, leathery bread crusts, and unrisen cakes were more com-

mon than not. Nina wasn't quite sure why they were
fighting the baking battle again, except that she had a
suspicion it had something to do with the mailman.

Ida had suggested that they bake cookies to give to the
building staff, the idea being that the sweets would make
a pair of twenties look a little plusher. The fact that the
mailman was Greek and that Nina was almost positive Ida
had some sort of a crush on him made the choice of
recipe less puzzling.

Nina was finding her task of shaping the cookies to be
meditatively soothing. The recipe called for the cookie to
be shaped around a whole clove, and there was something
satisfying about placing a small, perfectly shaped clove in
the dead center of the cookie. Since she had given up
puzzles as a small child and had never gotten around to
taking up tennis, flower arranging, or contact lenses, she
missed the feeling of achievement one got from perfect
placement.

"So what do you do when your partner is a *putz*," Ida
said, "and you don't want to work with him anymore?
They weren't married to each other, after all."

"Yeah, but I'm sure that a job divorce can be as painful
as the other kind."

"I guess so," Ida said. "You hear all the same stories
when partners break up—first they bring in the lawyers,
then they spend years in protracted litigation, and in the
end, everyone's life is ruined."

"I see you have a very rosy view of change."

"It's not my long suit." Ida was actually someone who
had blossomed while being trapped. If anybody could
conceivably have made the crumbling South Bronx work
for her, Ida had.

"Anyway," Nina said, "in this particular case, Elliott
got sole custody."

"Sounds like it."

"I guess that's what's puzzling me. It's like Andy walked away from his own child and never looked back."

"Oh, please," Ida said. "Leptin might be a very powerful chemical substance, but it was not his child."

"But he devoted his life to it. Years spent nurturing it, up all night in the lab, scrubbing racks of test tubes, heating up formula . . ."

"Nina, spare me the strained analogies. Or call your friend Ellen Simon. Maybe she'll pay you for them. I did tell you she called yesterday, didn't I?"

"Yeah, you did."

"Did you call her back?"

"Nope."

"Why not?"

"I don't know what to say to her. I haven't figured out a thing and I think I'm just using this murder as a way of not getting on with my life."

"A distinct possibility."

"But I'm so sick of getting on with my life. I've been getting on with my life . . . well, all my life."

"What's the alternative?" Ida sprinkled the latest batch of cookies with powdered sugar. She stepped back to admire her handiwork. "How do these look?" she asked.

"They look great. Maybe you and I should start a cookie business."

"Can you think of any two people more ill-suited for running a cookie business?"

"No."

"Say it with pride."

"Wait a minute," Nina said. "I'm not a total domestic failure. I'm proud to report that I have successfully buried every clove smack in the dead center of each cookie."

"You're a culinary genius. Then try cooking dinner every night for thirty years and see how far you get."

"While wearing a girdle."

"Right. I forgot about the girdle."

"Okay, you win," Nina said. "You've had a worse life than I have."

"You're only halfway there. You could still catch up."

"Well, I seem to be doing better on the pathetic scale. Unemployed, living with my mother, baking cookies for cheap thrills. But I'm falling behind on the depressed scale."

"In what way?" Ida asked.

"Nothing seems to bother me anymore. No boyfriend, no job, no apartment, but who cares? Can't button my skirt? Big deal. Only four hundred bucks left in my savings account? So what, it's better than nothing. I could go on like this forever. I think it might have something to do with coloring my hair. What do you think?"

"I think it might have more to do with dropping out of the race. You were always like that."

"Like what?"

"You were the kind of kid who hoped and prayed that you didn't get picked for a team. You were always happy to sit on the sidelines and watch. Competition was not your thing. It never has been."

"So I was really born to be a spinster living with my mother. And in a different century I'd be wrapping bandages and baking cookies and perfectly happy."

"Well, you're already baking cookies. And you claim to be perfectly happy. So wrap a few bandages and make your life complete."

Nina rolled another cookie around a clove. "I hate this holiday," she said. "Forty years of going to a movie and eating Chinese food."

"What else is a Jew supposed to do on Christmas Day?" Ida asked.

"Let's go out of town."

"That would be even more depressing."

"How come?" Nina said.

"Why go to a town where there aren't even enough Jews to fill up the local Chinese restaurant, not to mention the tenplex cinema at the mall."

"Well, do you have any ideas?"

"I have one."

"What is it?"

"We could go visit the Campbells."

It took Nina a minute to figure out that Ida was talking about Andy's parents. "You're right, I really should pay them a visit, shouldn't I?"

"Yes, I think it's time."

"All right, we'll bring Mr. and Mrs. Campbell some Christmas cookies. How's that?"

"As long as my mailman gets his."

"Don't worry, I wouldn't mess up your postal romance," Nina said. "Are you sure you want to come along? It's going to be freezing upstate."

"My dear, that's why God invented Thinsulate."

CHAPTER
TWENTY-SIX

"WHEN DID THEY SAY we should come by?" Nina asked her mother. Ida had handled the phone arrangements with the Campbells, since old ladies played so well out-of-town. Unlike in the city, where it sometimes felt as if they were bugs meant to be squashed flat.

"On the twenty-third. They're going to be tied up after that."

"What time?"

"They said to come after dinner. Around six."

The days when you could laugh at country bumpkins for early dining were over. All the movie stars now claimed, in their fitness books, that they never ate a morsel past four in the afternoon. These days there seemed to be something unwholesome about sitting down to red wine and paella at ten-thirty, even though it had seemed so cool when Nina was young and knocking around the Costa del Sol.

"So should we rent a car and drive back that night?" Nina asked. "Or should we stay over?"

"It's up to you. You're the driver. Do you mind driving in the dark?"

"Nah, I can handle it." Like most Manhattan women, Nina's driving skills had atrophied over the years, but she'd beaten back some of her phobia during her stay in Los Angeles. Ida still had a valid driver's license, but it was more of an affectation than anything else, convenient identification when a picture ID was required. She was more comfortable on the M104 bus than behind the wheel.

"So what'll it be?" Nina said. "Hertz or Rent-a-Wreck?"

"Whatever costs less."

Ida was cheap when it came to things like rental cars, yet Nina had seen her drop big bucks on some batik pillow she'd found in an open-air market in Indonesia, or on an amber necklace in Moscow. It depended on the commodity. Ida would never let a waiter throw out half a portion of anything. She'd have him wrap up the entire meal except for the leftover coffee to take home for the next day's lunch. She'd buy her grandchildren presents from the Chinese guy who came through the subway cars yelling "One dollar, one dollar" and then pick up a dinner check that Ken could afford far more easily than she could.

As it turned out, car rentals were tough to get during Christmas week, so Ida and Nina found themselves in a brand-new aerodynamically styled Taurus in a shade of red that might more appropriately coat a candy apple than a Ford.

The ride up the Taconic Parkway to Columbia County is scenic any time of the year. But two days before Christmas, with a light frosting all the way north of Riverdale, the view was picture-postcard perfect. From Croton on, New York looked much as it must have when the area was settled by the Dutch. Swept up in a sentiment of northern European Christianity, Nina began to feel self-conscious about the cookies in her bag, as if the clovey smell was somehow redolent of pagan blasphemy.

"I'm starving," Nina said, somewhere in the middle of Columbia County.

"There must be a decent diner around here."

"Yeah, there's one right off the highway. Near the Hudson exit."

"How do you know?"

"I used to be a professional weekend guest, when I was young and being a schnorrer still had some dignity attached to it."

The Chief Taghkanic Diner had a promising smell of grease, and Nina and Ida slipped into a booth with enthusiasm. Nina ordered a cheeseburger platter, her usual out-of-town lunch. Americans had made a fair amount of progress when it came to bread and vegetables, but they were still best when it came to grilling beef and frying potatoes.

Ida ordered a chef's salad, which Nina always considered a mistake. In a place like this you ran the risk of getting American cheese.

"So what did Mrs. Campbell sound like on the phone?" Nina asked.

"She said to call her Lou."

"What kind of a name is that? Like Lou Costello? Is she Italian?"

"I don't know. I would think that it's short for something. Lucinda, Lucille?"

"Maybe Louise."

"Yeah, she sounded like a Louise."

"What does a Louise sound like?"

"Pleasant and calm."

"Probably bakes cookies without cloves in them," Nina said.

"I'm sure she's baked a lot of cookies in her lifetime. With and without cloves."

"What's her husband's name? Is he called Lou also?"

"No, he's Bob."

"Bob and Lou Campbell. Babaloo. Cute."

The waitress arrived with their order, plus a complimentary plate of white bread. Nina pointed to Ida's salad. "I told you to watch out for American cheese."

"It's actually Swiss," Ida said, holding up a piece for inspection.

"It looks suspiciously yellow for Swiss. Must be from a different part of Switzerland."

"Must be. Lou Campbell gave me very explicit directions, but it sounded complicated. I hope we don't get lost."

"Everything sounds complicated when you're used to just walking up and down Broadway."

But the directions proved to be quite clear, and Nina and Ida managed to navigate the red Taurus without taking one wrong turn. The entrance to the Campbells' farm was easy to spot, since the turnoff was marked by a huge sign that proclaimed BOB AND LOU CAMPBELL WELCOME YOU TO SYCAMORE ESTATES, A HOMEOWNERS' ASSOCIATION. SALES OFFICE STRAIGHT AHEAD, 50 YARDS ON THE RIGHT. OFFERING BY PROSPECTUS ONLY. The sign was professionally done, with an attractive graphic representation of a sycamore tree gracing the lettering.

"Holy shit," Nina said. "What's all this?"

"I don't know. Lou said to go past the trailer up to the main house, but she didn't say anything about the trailer being a real estate sales office."

They drove past the large white trailer with its tidy red canopy and up to a freshly painted Dutch colonial that sat perched on a hill. "Nice house," Ida said.

"What do you know? You're from the Bronx. By the way, you see any sycamore trees?"

"What do I know? I'm from the Bronx."

They pulled up next to a Jeep Cherokee and walked over to the front door. It had a lovely Christmas wreath on it, an artfully designed mixture of holly, twigs, and

silver stars. Nina thought she might have recognized
Roz's handiwork. "What do you think?" she asked Ida. "A
Brillstein creation?"

"Very possibly."

Before they had a chance to ring the bell, Lou Campbell came to the door. She was dressed a little cornily, in a
white polyester blouse tucked into black polyester slacks.
But she wore a blue-and-white fleece jacket that was
made out of a pretty cool snowflake print. Her hair was
cut into a short gray fringe that could have been found on
any American farmer's wife, but could have just as easily
been worn by an extremely sophisticated elderly lesbian
novelist living on an island off the coast of Maine.

"Mrs. Fischman?" Lou addressed Ida and extended her
hand.

"Please call me Ida."

"Well, Ida, pleased to meet you. I'm Lou and you must
be Ida's daughter." She had a professional handshake.
Nina could imagine her selling real estate, despite the
synthetic blouse that tied in a bow at the neck.

"I'm Nina. Nice to meet you."

"Come inside. Bob's in the den. I'll tell him you're
here. Would you like something to drink? I already have a
pot of decaf on the stove."

Was it safe to assume that if it was a pot, then it was
brewed? People didn't make pots of instant coffee, did
they? "I'd love some," Nina said.

"Me too. We brought you some cookies," Ida said, offering the box in a Bloomingdale's shopping bag. Suddenly there seemed something terribly Jewish about
Bloomingdale's.

" 'Tis the season to bake," Nina said, trying to compen-
sate for the bag.

"Why, thank you." Lou led Nina and Ida into the living room and put them on the couch. "I'll be right back with Bob. Make yourselves comfortable."

As soon as Lou left, Nina got up to inspect the joint. The room seemed to have all the appropriate hallmarks of Americana—a braided rug, a plaid couch, a fireplace mantel that exhibited a respectable showing of Christmas cards. In the corner sat the Campbells' Christmas tree, decorated with an assortment of ornaments that ranged from tasteful antiques to luridly colored Power Rangers. On the coffee table sat a stack of offering prospectuses for Sycamore Estates. Nina inevitably succumbed to the impulse to flip through one. And just as inevitably, Bob Campbell walked in while she was perusing the contents.

CHAPTER
TWENTY-SEVEN

"INTERESTED IN BUYING a lot?" Bob Campbell asked.

"Oh, hi." Nina put the prospectus back on the coffee table.

"Hello, I'm Bob Campbell. Pleased to meet you." He shook both sets of extended hands. Campbell had the look of a small-town businessman rather than a farmer. It was a look you never saw in the city, where it seemed as though the more successful you were, the more paranoid and driven you became. He looked like a guy who had been doing business with the same people in the same way for his whole life. He was comfortable rather than smug, as if he knew what to expect and that it would all work out. He didn't look like a man who had just lost his son.

Lou walked into the living room carrying the Fischman family cookies on a platter lined with a paper doily. Nina had a friend who claimed that her mother had taught her never to let food touch a platter, that the dish should always be lined with something like doilies or lettuce leaves.

Ida Fischman, on the other hand, was not a woman who believed in extra layers. Her kids only wore undershirts when it was really cold out. There was enough dirty laundry in life already. And as far as doilies were concerned, she tried to stay away from anything white. The color reminded her of people who were trying too hard.

Nina, of course, hadn't come into contact with a doily since she stopped making Valentines in elementary school. She wouldn't know where to buy one if she had to. Did they come in six-packs in the supermarket or did you have to go to some specialty shop to buy them?

"So what brings you here for the holidays?" Lou asked, after she had made a quick trip back to the kitchen for the coffee.

"Actually, we came to see you," Nina said. "My sister and brother-in-law were very good friends of your son's. Needless to say, they were extremely affected by his death." She decided not to mention the fact that Ken had been suspected of some involvement in the murder.

"Yes, we've met Ken and Laura," Lou said.

"Is he the skin doctor?" Bob asked.

"Yes, dear," his wife replied. "Remember, they've been at all the children's birthday parties. Your daughter is so lovely," she said to Ida.

Nina knew that Lou was not talking about her when she used the word *lovely*. People always used that and similar adjectives to describe Laura. For Nina they veered toward *interesting* and *funny*. The kind of description that couldn't get you a blind date.

"Anyway," Nina said, "we came up here because we were all very puzzled by what happened to Andy. We thought that talking to both of you might make some things clearer. I've spoken to so many people—Andy's wife, his colleagues in the lab, the guy he used to do research with. None of them really was able to contribute much in the way of solving this . . . um . . . mystery, if you will."

"We thought," Ida said, "that maybe you, as his par-

ents, could give us some kind of an overview of his life
that might point up something we've overlooked."

Bob and Lou Campbell sat quietly in the two wing
chairs facing the couch. They looked thoughtful rather
than sad. It was a reaction that a Jew would have been
embarrassed to have, considering the circumstances. *Ges-
chrei* was not an active verb around these parts. But
whether this meant anything significant, Nina could not
tell.

Lou finally spoke. "You know, we were never happy
about Andy's moving to New York City. But we knew
from an early age that we'd never be able to keep him
here. He was so smart, ever since he was a tiny baby.
That's why Bob and I decided to go ahead and send him
to Cornell."

"I had hoped," Bob said, "that the Ag school might get
him interested in the farm. But from the beginning he
spent all his time in the lab. And it just confirmed what I
had really known all along. That I had lost him."

They had lost him in so many ways, Nina thought. By
sending him away to college, by having him move to the
city and marry a Jew. Death was, of course, the ultimate
loss. Perhaps the Campbells' composure was due to the
fact that they had so much practice in grieving over the
years.

"Do you have other children?" Nina asked.

"We have three daughters," Lou said.

"Do they live around here?"

"There's only one left in the county. And she lives in
Hudson." Lou said the name of the town as if it were a
euphemism for something. Probably, Nina suspected, for
giving birth to biracial children and collecting welfare.

Daughters were supposed to stick around. That was the
point of them. The good ones married within the tribe
(or not at all), moved nearby (or not at all), gave you

grandchildren to bounce on your knee, or else nursed you in your old age. They weren't supposed to move out of the county. But then, you weren't supposed to carve up the family farm into single-home lots.

"So you're selling off some land?" Nina asked.

"All of it," Bob said. "After we've sold the land, we're going to sell this house."

"And move where?"

"There's a Winnebago we've been saving for. Even before we decided to subdivide the farm, we had set up a savings account. Our Winnie fund, we call it. Lou and I are going to hit the road."

Nina had seen elderly American couples at places like the Grand Canyon who had rolled their lives up into an Airstream trailer. They all claimed to be totally happy, to not miss a thing. She always wondered how they avoided the plague of chronic constipation.

"How interesting," Ida said. "It sounds like so much fun."

"Do you like to travel?" Lou asked.

"Oh, yes. I went to Peru last year and had a very wonderful time."

"We can't wait," Bob said. "Deep-sea fishing in the Gulf, then up to the mountains for some trout. We're even thinking of going all the way up to Alaska to catch some salmon." His gaiety didn't sound false, but his expression, if not apprehensive, was at least impassive.

"Do you fish also?" Nina asked Lou.

"Oh, sure." She didn't seem to be about to expand on that, so Nina gave her mother the kind of silent signal that meant "do something."

"As Nina has said, she spoke to a lot of the people in Andy's life. And she can't seem to get any kind of a lead on who might have wanted your son dead. As parents, of course, we're all very protective of our children. Even after they grow up. That's why I thought that a mother or father might be the perfect person to have sensed danger at some point in your son's life. And that sense could possibly give us some clue as to what happened."

"Well, of course, there are plenty of people that Andy hooked up with that we didn't exactly approve of, you know." Bob's lips formed an R, but he choked back the word. Nina wondered what it would be like to have Roz as a daughter-in-law. Especially if you were Bob.

"Our son created a life for himself that we didn't always understand," Lou said, "but we never told him what to do. When it came to marriage and career, we told ourselves that we just had to trust his judgment."

"Actually, the people he was working with in the lab lately seemed very nice." Bob gave a slight emphasis to the word *lately*. It was pronounced enough, however, to sufficiently vilify Elliott.

"And of course, we love our grandchildren very much," Lou added. "We hope that we're not going to have any problem in continuing to see them."

If the Campbells had been Jewish, really Jewish, like the kind that Nina had grown up with, this conversation would have progressed further. Bob would have been starting his sentences with "that daughter-in-law of mine" and Lou would already be in tears, protesting that the whole thing was not her fault. But the Campbells were not Jewish and their living room was in Columbia County, not Bayside, and Nina just couldn't quite figure out how to open them up.

Lou reached over and tried a cookie. "These really are delicious. You know, Roz is a great baker too. She makes the best pies."

Was that the problem? Did the Campbells see the Fischmans as part of a global Jewish conspiratorial baking cabal?

"You know, Nina, I just had a thought," Lou said. "Andy left a lot of personal papers with us."

"He did?"

"Yes, I assume they were things that he chose not to share with Roz."

"I see." There was a graciousness to Lou's reticence, Nina thought. *Chose not to share* was such a kinder phrase than most would use. There was no point in being inflammatory and indulging in words like *grubby little paws* when your relationship with your grandchildren was at stake. Lou was a sensible woman and her husband was going along with her. There was nothing wrong with that. Why charge in here and try to rip all that asunder?

"I haven't had the heart to go through his things yet," Lou said. "Perhaps you'd like to take a look. There could be something there that might be helpful to you."

"Are you sure you don't mind?" Ida asked. "We didn't come up here to invade your privacy."

"No, I think it would be all right. Don't you, Bob?"

"Yeah, sure, fine." He seemed far away. Perhaps he was already mentally trolling for marlin off the Florida Keys. Or, more likely, mourning in his own controlled way the loss of his only son and of his only farm.

"I've been keeping the boxes in the attic," Lou said. "I'm afraid it's a bit of a climb." She looked at Ida.

"Oh, I think I can still manage a flight of stairs," she said. "It can't be as bad as Machu Picchu."

CHAPTER
TWENTY-EIGHT

THE CAMPBELLS' ATTIC looked more like an office than a storage space. There were two antique desks, and one wall was lined with wooden filing cabinets.

"Look at all this oak," Ida said. "How gorgeous."

"Oh, these are all things we picked up at auction," Lou said. "Except for this desk. It was my grandfather's."

Life in America was good. People had grandfathers who owned desks, and attics to put them in. The existence eked out by the folk who inhabited that grandiose shtetl known as Manhattan seemed meager by comparison.

"What a beautiful piece." Ida appraised it with the eye of a dealer. She gently ran her fingers around every little compartment and lowered and raised the rolltop a few times. Nina was always surprised when her mother exhibited any appreciation for old-fashioned decorative items, since traditionalism was something tainted rather than exalted, to Ida. It was a generational thing—all of Ida's friends from Hunter College had that attitude. They had turned their backs on their parents' orthodoxy and had simultaneously rejected anything carved, brocaded, or ornate in any manner. Stark modernism was their religion.

But every now and then Ida would go mad for something so *ungepotchket* that it made Nina wonder. Her mother's adamant admiration for the occasional ruby-encrusted tiara seemed to have more significance than just a lapse of taste. It was as if she was arguing against the Young Communist League organizer who, one day in 1938, turned Ida in a certain direction and made her leave behind the possibility of rubies and golden oak pigeonholes forever.

"Nice desk," Nina said, with neutral emotion. She was, after all, homeless at the moment and wasn't even in a position to take sides. Tubular steel and refinished rolltops both exceeded her grasp.

"Andy's things are all in that file cabinet over there," Lou said. "But I'm afraid I have no idea what kind of filing system he used. When he said that he wanted to leave some papers with me, I just gave him the key to the cabinet and he dumped all his stuff in himself."

"And he let you keep the key."

"I have a duplicate."

"Did he know that?"

"I assume he did. We never discussed it. Besides, I never looked to see what was in there."

"Probably his prenuptial agreement," Nina said.

"I don't think he had a prenuptial agreement. But I assume that some of his papers do concern financial matters that he did not want to share with Roz." Lou was stating a fact, not dripping with triumphant venom. An admirable pose, but was her calm reasonableness hiding something?

Lou handed Ida the key. "Please, can you do this on your own? I'm not really ready for this. I'll be downstairs if you decide you need me."

"Are you sure that you feel okay about all this?" Ida asked. "Because if you'd rather we held off . . ."

"No, no. Obviously I'm anxious to get to the bottom of all this. Please go ahead."

"Okay."

Lou went back downstairs, and Ida handed Nina the

key. She made a move toward the file cabinet, and then hesitated.

"What's the matter?" Ida asked.

"Sometimes I think I should just mind my own business."

"And then the feeling passes."

"I guess."

"Good. Minding your own business is so limiting."

"People do it."

"They have a different genetic constitution."

Nina laughed.

"It's true," Ida said. "Even when you were a little baby, you always kept track of everyone else. One New Year's Eve, I think you were maybe four at the most, we gave a big party and everyone dumped their coats on the bed. You were able to match up each guest with their coat. It was truly amazing."

"So I'm a genius when it comes to what? How could you classify that talent?"

"I don't know."

"What do you grow up to be when you can match people with their coats?"

"A yenta?"

"That's right. I'm a natural-born yenta. It's my birthright, so here we are, more than a hundred miles from home, going through someone else's file cabinet because . . . because . . . because why?"

"Because it's there," Ida said. She took the key from Nina and fitted it into the lock on the top of the cabinet.

Fifteen minutes later, Nina turned to her mother. "This is the most boring set of files I've ever trespassed upon."

"We're not trespassing. Besides, what did you expect? What would I find if I broke into your personal file cabinet? Stacks of torrid love letters wrapped in satin ribbons and scented with lavender water?"

"Hardly. My personal correspondence is not of the variety that will ever need to be burned. In fact, I have no personal correspondence. Unless you count the Internal Revenue Service and Citibank."

"Look at this." Ida was flipping through a file marked SWANSONG.

"What is it?"

"Papers relating to the breakup."

"What breakup?"

"The breakup of Elliott and Andy's research team."

"What's there?"

"A few memos. Some letters. And there's something that looks like a contract."

"Let me see."

"Okay, you're the lawyer."

"Oh, right," Nina said. "I forgot."

"You certainly did."

"Yeah, I better remember before I spend every cent in my bank account."

"No comment." Ida handed over the file.

"Hmmm." Nina scanned the contract the way she usually perused legal documents—at top speed, trying to avoid getting bogged down by the boring boilerplate. She often missed things by using this cursory method, but at least it got her to the end.

"What does it say?" Ida asked.

"You won't believe this."

"What?"

"I can't believe this."

"What?"

"Well, this explains a lot."

"What?"

"It speaks volumes."

"Nina, you're not funny. In fact, you're getting extremely annoying."

"Okay, okay. This is an agreement between Elliott and Andy that was entered into upon the dissolution of their partnership. It guarantees Andy a third of all future earnings from the marketing of leptin."

"Really?"

"And there's a side agreement wherein Elliott agrees not to tell Roz about any of this." Nina felt a little silly using *wherein* when talking to her mother. But she wasn't trying to be pretentious, it just came out. Besides, she had a sneaking suspicion that it made Ida feel like at least something had come out of all that law school tuition money that the Fischmans had coughed up.

"That man really didn't want his wife to know anything about his finances, did he?"

"I guess not. First the apartment building in Borough Park and now this."

"Could Roz have had that big a problem? Or was Andy just paranoid?"

"Maybe both. But it's hard not to assume that she was the crazy one." It made Nina wonder how so many successful marriages could be built on acceptance of the fact that one of the spouses was a lunatic. All those years of going to therapy to become sane was probably a total waste of time if her goal had been to marry herself off.

"Does it say anything about what happens upon the death of either of the parties?" Ida asked.

"Let's see. No, it doesn't. It's a very homemade document. I think they drafted it themselves. Elliott probably copied it from something his brother-in-law the dentist gave him."

"What brother-in-law the dentist?"

"He seems," Nina said, "like the kind of guy who would have a brother-in-law who's a dentist, doesn't he?"

"Yeah, he does. Anyway, with Andy dead and Roz probably ignorant of the existence of this agreement, there's no way to enforce the contract, is there?"

"Well, the contract would still be enforceable by the estate, as long as it doesn't provide otherwise," Nina said.

"But someone would have to know about it before they could enforce it."

"True."

"And besides us," Ida said, "who knows about it?"

"Elliott."

"And there's no reason on earth that Elliott would want to enforce it, is there?"

"Nope." Nina put the file back on top of the antique oak cabinet.

"So as long as Andy stays dead, Elliott gets to keep his mouth shut and hold on to all the money."

"Right."

"Sounds like a motive for murder to me."

"So what do we do about it?"

Ida didn't say anything, but gave Nina one of those clean-up-your-room looks.

"What do you want from my life?" Nina asked. "Besides grandchildren."

"I guess you'll have to talk to Elliott."

"Yech."

"Yeah, well, I don't think you have much of a choice."

"What if he won't see me?"

"I think you should surprise him. You know, not give him a chance to avoid you."

"It's not my style," Nina said. "I don't know if I can pull it off."

"I'll go with you." Ida patted her daughter on her forearm. "We'll corner him. Two against one."

"When should we do this?"

"As soon as possible. How about Christmas Day?"

"Christmas Day?"

"Yeah, Christmas," Ida said. "Why not? Are you doing anything else?"

"No."

"It's perfect. I'm sure he'll be home. We can sneak in with the Chinese deliveryman."

"What if he's not home?" Nina said. "He not only seems like the kind of guy who has a brother-in-law who's a dentist, but also a wife who's a Christian."

"We'll find him."

"What if we can't?"

"Nina, don't whine," Ida whined.

CHAPTER
TWENTY-NINE

ELLIOTT MADE IT EASY for them. He was listed in the Manhattan telephone directory. Ida and Nina called his home number as soon as they got back to the city, despite the late hour. They got his answering machine. He had left the kind of detailed message that narcissists just can't resist. "I'm out of town for a few days," his tape reported. "I'm sorry that I can't tell you where. But believe me, it's going to be an interesting trip. I'll be back on Christmas Eve, although the way things look, I'll probably have to spend the holiday in the lab. But leave a message, and I'll get back to you as soon as my schedule permits."

"I thought he had a wife," Nina said to Ida.

"Maybe she has her own answering machine."

"Probably. More proof of my original theory."

"Which is?"

"Elliott Adler has no sharing skills."

"I'm sure that showed up consistently on all of his elementary school report cards. But I doubt whether they'll be admissible at trial," Ida said.

"Depends on whether he testifies."

"If his answering machine is any indication, I'd say he'll take the stand."

"So what do we do next?" Nina asked.

"We'll have to pay a visit to the lab."

"On Christmas Day?"

"Why, are you busy?"

"Of course not. Why should this year be any different from any other year?" Sometimes Nina suspected that Jews married Christians just so they'd have something to do on December twenty-fifth for once in their lives.

"So what's the problem?"

"How are we going to get into the lab on Christmas? Won't everything be locked up tight?"

"So we'll sneak in." Ida made it sound like a fun suggestion, like a trip to the discount outlets in Secaucus. Actually, it was probably easier to sneak into Elliott's lab than it was to get to the Searle outlet without a car.

"How are we going to sneak in?"

"We'll have to take someone into our confidence," Ida said. "Someone who works there."

"Tina." Of course.

"Better than the other one?" Ida asked.

"David? He's a pill."

"And she's not?"

"Not at all."

"You think she's up for this?"

"I do. I just hope that we're able to reach her. She's probably on vacation or something."

"Well, let's try." Tina was listed as well, and they got her answering machine also. Hers was a far more humble message than Elliott's. "You've reached 555-6943. Please leave a message at the tone and we'll get back to you."

We. Nina knew single women who made sure that they used the word *we* on their tape, just to make themselves sound less vulnerable. In recent years, New Yorkers had become more casual about answering machines, but in the beginning they had been very wary. You weren't supposed to record a message stating that you weren't in right now. You could, however, say that you weren't available, indicating that you were there to guard your turf, but you were using the hair dryer and couldn't hear the phone ring.

One guy she knew had recorded a message that ran: "I can't come to the phone right now because I'm sitting on the toilet with a shotgun on my lap. That's my ferocious Doberman you hear in the background." And then he barked. It was funny at first, but then, like all clever messages, it got annoying after a while and he had to change it to something more staid.

Nina left a brief message, reminding Tina of who she was, and got a call back thirty minutes later.

"Hi, it's Tina."

"Oh, thanks for calling."

"What's this all about? I mean, your message sounded so mysterious."

"We think we might know who murdered Andy. And we need your help to prove it."

"Let me guess."

"Go ahead."

"Elliott."

"Oh, Jesus, here I am, running around, taking the D train all the way out to Brooklyn, buying Roz Brillstein grilled vegetable sandwiches, trying to stumble upon some clue that would help me solve this murder. And you knew all along."

"Well, I didn't *know*," Tina said. "I just suspected."

"What made you suspect him?"

"How could I not?"

"I guess I see your point. Anyway, after all this schlepping around, I finally paid a visit to Andy's parents."

"In Columbia County?"

"Yup."

"That's funny. You're complaining about taking the D train to Brooklyn, but not about going all the way up-state?"

"Yeah, well, I'm an IRT person."

"I hear you."

"So I went up to talk to the Campbells and the wife let me go through some of Andy's stuff that he stored there." Nina gave Tina a basic description of the document she had found. "Did you know that such a thing existed?"

Tina thought for a moment. "Now that you mention it, it makes sense."

"Why?"

"Well, David and I were always amazed at how accepting Andy seemed of Elliott's success. He never succumbed to murderous rages of jealousy, the way I would have. Andy seemed to come to terms with the fact that Elliott was going to be rich and famous. Suspiciously accepting, I would say, knowing what I know now."

"Did you ever ask him how come he was able to handle the whole thing so well?"

"No, I just figured that Andy was a better person than me. Someone who cared more about science than about amassing personal wealth."

"Yeah, well, I guess you were wrong," Nina said.

"Maybe there's no such thing."

"There must be people like that. But I don't think that any of them are married to Roz Brillstein."

"I see your point."

"So I had this idea," Nina said. "I made a photocopy of the agreement. I thought that if I caught Elliott off guard, alone in the lab, maybe I'd get him to confess."

"Elliott's never off guard. His life is just one big public relations opportunity."

"I think it's worth a try. Would you be willing to let us in to the lab on Christmas Day?"

"Us? Who's us?"

"Well, actually, I'm bringing my mother."

"Your mother?"

"Yeah. It's been my experience that she makes excellent camouflage."

"Right," Tina said. "No one looks at old ladies in New York, do they?"

"Never."

"Okay, I'll be glad to help you out. I wouldn't mind seeing Elliott Adler hauled off to a life sentence. Meet me at ten in the morning on the northeast corner of Sixty-fifth Street and York Avenue, okay?"

"You're on."

"Nina, could you do me one favor?"

"What's that?"

"I'd rather you didn't tell anyone about my involvement. The whole thing will cause quite a scandal at the university."

"Fine with me. And Tina, I hope this isn't going to interfere with your plans for Christmas Day."

"Not at all. My family doesn't celebrate the holiday. We just go to the movies and eat Chinese food."

Nina laughed. She continually had to remind herself that Jews did not necessarily corner the market on alienation.

CHAPTER THIRTY

NINA AND IDA HAD DRESSED in the most threatening manner they could manage. Perhaps Nina was subconsciously aping the juvenile delinquents of her youth, because in addition to dressing in black, she stopped on the corner and bought a pack of Dentyne. Chewing gum made her feel tougher, even though Dentyne was not a particularly tough brand. Ida donned her usual New Balance running shoes, worn for comfort, not for swiftness. She also wore a smocky navy blue top that could possibly trigger memories of Elliott's kindergarten teacher and therefore serve to infantilize and intimidate him.

Tina was already waiting for them on the corner, and she whisked them past building security and up into Elliott's lab without any trouble. "You can let yourselves out, can't you?" she asked.

"Sure."

"Okay. See you." She pointed them in the direction of Elliott and then disappeared. Nina looked at the expanse of lab that stretched out before them. Her heels clicked against the vinyl tile floor as she walked.

"I feel like I'm being played by Sigourney Weaver," she said to Ida, "in one of those creepy movies."

"Yeah, I feel like I could definitely use a little bit more height."

"Do you think he's dangerous?"

"It's hard to think of someone named Elliott Adler as dangerous," Ida said. "But I suppose anything is possible. I don't know, I haven't met him."

They walked down the hall toward Elliott's lab cautiously. Suddenly their silence was punctured by a voice behind them. "Ladies?" Elliott boomed. "May I help you?"

They both froze in mid-step. He walked around to face them. He was wearing a white lab coat, which swung open over a black turtleneck. The effect was sinister.

"Merry Christmas, Dr. Adler," Nina said.

He didn't move a facial muscle in response.

"Hello, I'm Ida Fischman." She extended her hand. "Nice to meet you."

He took her hand in spite of himself and gave it a begrudging shake. "Elliott Adler. Nice to meet you," he muttered.

"Well, you must be wondering what brings us here," Ida said. It was clearly going to have to be her show. The kindergarten teacher routine seemed to be working. She forged ahead, not waiting for an answer. "Why don't we all sit down somewhere. I think it's time we had a chat."

"Okay." He obviously didn't know what else to say. "Come on into my office."

"Thank you," said Mrs. Fischman, brisk and efficient.

They followed him down the hall, mother slightly in front of daughter. Nina was glad that her mother was here, relieved that Ida seemed to instinctively know how to handle him. But sometimes Nina felt impatient, wondering when the hell her mother was going to get senile already.

Things had been easier back in the Bronx, when Ida had lacked the glamor of the other neighborhood moms, the ones who had married right out of high school and clomped around in high-heeled mules. "I will never wear space shoes," Nina had sworn.

The space shoe had been replaced by New Balance, which everyone wore, thereby eliminating Nina's ability to transcend her mother via footwear. And lately the fact that Nina had slept with more men than her mother ever had was no longer a source of comfort. Because Ida, who had seemed old before her time at forty, had remained alert, competent, and even youthful in her own unglamorous way.

And Nina was getting sick of it. She continually found herself monitoring Ida for signs of impending dementia. Not because she worried about getting her on the list for the Hebrew Home for the Aged, but simply to make herself feel better.

But Ida never seemed to lock herself out of her apartment or miss a payment on her Visa bill. Occasionally she'd grope for a word. "Here I am," Ida would say, "becoming a member of the C.R.A.F.T. club. Can't Remember a Fucking Thing."

Even the fact that her seventy-five-year-old mother could say *fuck* without flinching annoyed Nina. And here Ida was, handling Elliott like a . . . what was the expression? Like a rug? Like a baby? Like a glove? Nina couldn't remember. Perhaps she was ready to apply for C.R.A.F.T. membership herself.

Elliott sat himself behind his desk and motioned them both into the two seats that faced him. He looked stern and impatient but also interested. As if he were a family therapist dealing with an incurable couple.

"Now," Ida began, practically shaking her finger at him, using her own stern and impatient voice. "I want you to know that Nina and I have been up to our usual, sticking our noses into other people's business."

"It's what we're good at," Nina offered.

"There's no need to explain or apologize," Ida said sharply. "We were asked to make some inquiries and we did. And what we found was simply shocking."

"And what was that?" Elliott tried to put a sneer in his voice, but he sounded whipped.

"My daughter Laura and her husband happen to have been very good friends of Andy Campbell's. And after Andy was *murdered*, there were some allegations that my son-in-law might have been involved. Our family felt it incumbent upon ourselves to prove otherwise. My daughter Nina, with some assistance from myself, has conducted a thorough investigation into the circumstances surrounding the murder. And guess what?"

"What?" You could barely hear him.

"You're the only person with a motive."

"Me? What kind of motive do I have?" Elliott didn't sound the least bit convincing. He tried to smirk, but couldn't pull it off.

Ida dug into her ever-present Channel 13 tote bag and produced a copy of the document that they had photocopied upstate. "Does this seem like sufficient motive to you?" she snapped. "Because it does to me."

Elliott whimpered audibly.

"Not only that," Ida continued, "but you had sufficient opportunity. The day before he was murdered, Andy spent the entire time in the lab drinking coffee."

"So?"

"Coffee that you had laced with methanol. A substance that typically takes a while to kick in and left him dead in his bed the following morning."

Ida stood up and leaned over him. She somewhat managed to tower, despite her mere sixty-two inches. Her feat was made easier by the fact that Elliott remained sitting.

Sitting and practically sucking his thumb. "I don't know what you're talking about," he said, sounding totally lame, like some kid claiming that the dog ate his homework.

"I don't believe you." Now Ida was towering and thundering. "I know a liar when I see one. Believe me, I didn't teach school all those years and not develop some instinct for weeding out veracity. And the lack thereof."

Nina was very impressed. She was used to thinking of Ida as the oppressed schoolteacher/mother who stumbled around the house washing dishes and folding laundry and writing all those goddamn plan books into the night in her small and neat repressed handwriting.

Nina had never seen her towering and thundering. Perhaps there was a payoff after all to indulging in several decades of psychotherapy. Or perhaps (and this was the cheaper alternative) the fact that you didn't have to go on dates or job interviews anymore put your superego and id into such a balance that you could scream at rich, successful men who were on their third wives. Scream without apology, without secretly hoping that they would ask you out afterward, even if they were murderers. Nina decided to give it a try.

"Elliott," she began, in as snotty a tone as she could muster, "I'm sure you didn't start out this way. I'm sure that it took years for you to turn into a greedy pig. And years more to become a greedy pig who was capable of murder."

"I don't know what you're talking about." This time Elliott managed to sneer without any problem. Ida was clearly better at this than Nina.

"Okay," Ida said, trying to recover the ground that they had just lost, "cut the shit. We're turning this over to the police." She waved the document in front of his nose. "So if I were you, I'd get the name of a really good criminal attorney."

Elliott's eyes involuntarily flickered over toward his Rolodex.

"Actually, you probably already have one. You must have been expecting this for a while now."

"Not really."

"No?" Ida's contempt level hit a new high. Nina could just picture her in the front of a classroom.

"No, not like this." He gestured lamely toward mother and daughter.

"Well, we've already shown your little agreement to enough people, so that if anything happens to either of us, the proper authorities will be informed. So, Elliott," Ida hissed, "I wouldn't try anything funny."

"I wouldn't dream of it." Nina could tell that he really meant it.

CHAPTER
THIRTY-ONE

ELLEN SIMON LOOKED the way she always did, overgroomed and smiling. Her hair seemed to have been freshly highlighted, as if she had just put an extra glint of gold in it right before lunch. She wore it tousled, with bangs. The bangs were never too short or too long, intimating that they must have been trimmed within the week. The nails never had a chip, the stockings never had a run, the skin never had a blemish. And Ellen was always so damn perky. She either took iron supplements or drank human blood for breakfast; Nina was never sure which was the case.

Ellen wore a red suit with a black velvet collar and cuffs. The outfit was a little too Christmasy for a Jewish girl to be wearing this time of year. But it looked quite agreeable next to ruby earrings and the large cabochon ring. And her nail polish matched her ring exactly.

"Nina, it's so good to see you." Ellen was waiting at the table when Nina got there.

They were at the Union Square Café. Nina had been there once before, for someone's birthday. It had been hard to get reservations for dinner. She wondered if it was equally difficult at lunch. She did not have to wonder long.

"It was hell getting a table," Ellen said, "especially around the holidays. There are so many tourists in town."

She waved the imaginary tourists away, as if swatting at flies.

The restaurant had a graceful informality. The flowers looked like something you would have on your own table, the waiters looked like people you might have gone to graduate school with. The message was that the stuffy old guard was out, that we had taken over the world. And now we're charging you prices that you can't afford unless you're on an expense account.

It was obvious that Ellen was. A large bottle of Pellegrino sat on the table, signifying that someone else was picking up the tab.

"You look great," Nina said, "as always."

"So do you." Ellen carefully examined Nina's hair, without trying to hide her scrutiny.

"It's dark, isn't it?" Nina tried not to sound too apologetic.

"It's interesting with your blue eyes. Sort of makes you look Irish."

"Is that good?"

"Of course it's good. Not looking Jewish is a whole industry, for chrissakes."

"Well, I didn't do it to look Irish," Nina said. "I did it to look more colorful."

"And you do. But that's not the only thing that's colorful," she said, leaning in toward Nina. "I just loved your piece. So funny. I had no idea." Ellen's tone, of course, was mildly insulting. As if Nina was some nerdy chem major in a B movie who takes off her glasses, lets down her hair, and turns out to give fabulous blow jobs.

"It was great fun to work on such a good story," Nina said. "With such describable characters. I wish you could meet Roz, for example."

"Or Elliott." Ellen wiped an imaginary speck of something off her cuff.

"Believe me, you don't want to meet Elliott."

"Well," Ellen said, "he's probably not going to be available for meetings. I understand that he was arrested the day before yesterday."

"Is that true? How did you hear that?"

"Oh, I have my sources."

Apparently better ones than Nina had. Despite the fact that Nina had been cooperating with the police, making herself available on an around-the-clock basis for the past week. "They arrested him for Andy's murder?" she asked.

"That's right."

"Based on the agreement they both signed?"

"That and a little bit more." Ellen went after another imaginary speck.

"Like what?"

"Oh, something they dug up after they got a search warrant and went through his stuff."

"Poison?"

"Well, sort of. They found some notes scribbled in a book next to a description of methanol. And also some residue in the lab. In Elliott's office."

"Really. So I didn't make this all up. It wasn't just a psychotic delusion."

"Oh no, not at all. You were right on the money." Ellen picked up the menu and examined its contents.

"Something to drink?" The waitress looked as though she might have a second job as a law librarian or a speech pathologist.

"Yeah, I could use a glass of wine. Red, I think," Nina said, being daring. Red wine was the last dangerous substance Nina permitted herself to ingest. It had all sorts of potential unpleasant side effects, like headaches and stained tooth enamel and an unsightly red nose, even though her rosacea had subsided since her visit to Ken.

But in the dead of winter, when the days were at their shortest, Nina found a strong red wine comforting.

"We have a lovely house merlot from a small winery in Oregon. Would you like to try it?"

"Sure." How bad could something from Oregon be? Such a wholesome place.

"I envy you," Ellen said, after the waitress had run off to fetch the wine.

Nina didn't dare ask why. She was sure that Ellen was going to say something mean, like she envied the fact that Nina could drink wine at lunch without worrying about its effect on her afternoon's productivity.

Even though Nina kept quiet and didn't bite, Ellen forged on. "I envy you because you're so unencumbered." She paused for Nina to respond.

"Unencumbered?" Nina felt compelled to say.

"Yes. While the rest of us were out there acquiring things like . . . you know . . . husbands and mortgages and private school tuition bills, you were just hanging out, being . . . I don't know . . . true to thine own self, I guess."

"Well, I don't know how accurate an assessment that is. Rich married people aren't the only ones who have to make compromises in this world." Nina reached for the glass of merlot that the waitress held and gulped at it while it was still in midair. "Don't think that you have cornered the market on personal sacrifice."

Ellen's laugh was closer to a bark than a tinkle. "Oh, Nina, you're too much."

Relieved that Ellen didn't appear to be offended, Nina finally let her glass touch down on the table. "So do you think you can use the material that I sent you?"

"Use it? Of course I can use it. Once we get an update on Elliott's status, you'll do a rewrite and we'll turn it into one of those juicy features that can run pages and pages.

If *The New Yorker* doesn't want it, I'll bet that we'll have no trouble selling it to *Vanity Fair*."

"You think so?"

"I know so. They'll love all that mad scientist stuff. People love to read about psychotic diet doctors."

"Elliott's not exactly a diet doctor. He's more of a research scientist."

"Oh, please. Don't you think he was already looking at office space on Park Avenue?"

"Yeah, I can see that."

"He probably had a literary agent who was shopping his book around."

"Well, Ellen, I'm very flattered that you found my article usable. It's really my first attempt."

"Don't sell yourself short." Ellen leaned over and held a hank of Nina's hair up against her own hand. "You really are an original. Dyeing your hair that color was absolute genius. You look like that actor, what's his name? The guy who used to be married to Ellen Barkin."

"Gabriel Byrne."

"Right, Gabriel Byrne. Nina, how do you think I would look if I did my hair that color?"

Nina knew that Ellen would look terrible. Her green eyes and tawny skin cried out for gold, not chestnut. But Nina had also learned a thing or two since she had turned forty. "Ellen, you'd look absolutely fabulous."

"Really?"

"Really. Just like Caroline Kennedy."

"You think so?"

"I do."

"You know, I could use someone like you assisting me with my column. I'm sure I could get you a decent salary. Not six figures, of course, but closer than not."

"Oh." Nina didn't exactly know what "closer than not" meant, but it sounded good to her.

Ellen gave a small pout. "Of course, it would mean cashing in a lot of chips, but I think it would be worth it. What do you think?"

Nina knew that Ellen would never have bothered to hire her if she hadn't been taken with her hair color. And that one day Ellen would decide that she didn't want a brunette around, and Nina would be replaced by a strawberry blonde. These were things that she knew, carefully noted, and then pushed aside as she picked up her wine and lifted it in Ellen's direction as she said, "Ellen, I think it would be absolutely fabulous."

CHAPTER
THIRTY-TWO

"OH MY GOD, I don't believe my eyes."

"What?" Ida said.

"Look." Nina pointed across the room. "It's Roz Brillstein and Peter Slater. And he's got his arm around her."

It was New Year's Day. Laura and Ken were having an open house in their Brooklyn brownstone. There was a lot of mulled wine and herbed breads and tons of people. It seemed that every mortgagor in Park Slope was pouring into the front hallway and searching for somewhere to put their leather bomber jackets.

Nina had her feet up on a settee in the corner, playing the elderly, mustachioed aunt that didn't quite understand the language. The effort of listening to any further discussion of the drawbacks of P.S. 321 was more than she could bear. Ida was the popular one at this party, keeping track of everyone's children's names and occasionally clearing away some of the tasteful, non-Christmasy patterned paper plates that Laura had bought on sale at the Metropolitan Museum of Art.

But Ida abandoned the trash can to sit down next to Nina's feet for the moment, just before Nina caught a glimpse of Roz's distinctive profile across the room.

"What is going on?" Nina asked.

"I don't know." Ida looked around the room. "Let me get Laura." She crossed over to where her daughter was

accepting compliments about her homemade focaccia.
"And she grows her own rosemary," Ida said, and pulled
Laura over to Nina's corner of the room.

"What's this about?" Laura asked. She was wearing a
buffalo plaid jumper that would have looked corny on
anyone with curves. But in combination with Laura's
thinness, chunky black boots, and a loop of hand-carved
ebony beads, she managed to make the outfit look more
downtown than Connecticut.

"Nice jumper," Nina said.

"Thanks. Catalog." Since Laura had started selling real
estate, she had affected the brisk, strained voice of a
working woman. "No time to shop, just to dial."

"Yeah, well, did Mom tell you that I just got a job?"
The saga of Roz and Peter would have to wait. The Fischman sisters' power balance was in need of immediate adjustment, as far as Nina was concerned.

"You did? Doing what?"

"Writing." Nina tried to sound archly casual, like Dorothy Parker when she was sober.

"Writing what?" Laura sounded nasty and contemptuous, like Dorothy Parker when she was drunk.

"A column."

"A column?"

"Well, not my own column. Helping Ellen Simon with
hers. You know who she is. The woman I've been working
for on the murder investigation."

"That vulture you went to high school with?" Laura
had definitely changed since she started working. She was
drifting away from her former plaid jumper self. Soon
she'd have to get an entirely new wardrobe of stiletto
heels, Bulgari jewelry, and spandex skirts.

"Yes, that vulture I went to high school with. She's got
a syndicated column and she needs a research assistant."

"So you're giving up law for writing?" Laura said. "Jesus, Nina, you'll be living with Mom forever."

Forget the Bulgari jewelry. Substitute a dog collar with spikes. Nina could see it all now—Laura would highlight her previously brown hair while Nina would go darker and darker. Finally they'd swap wardrobes. Then Laura would go off to law school and move the family to Manhattan. Nina would move to Brooklyn and begin spending more and more time perusing focaccia recipes. One day Laura would give Nina her three children to raise and the switch would be complete.

"Aren't you going to miss practicing law?" Laura asked.

"About as much as your children miss the head lice they had last spring."

Laura just shook her head sadly, as if she were the older sister instead of Nina. They were already beginning to live each other's lives.

"Listen," Nina said. "What's Roz Brillstein doing over there in the corner with Peter Slater?"

Laura watched the couple for a moment. "They appear to be kissing."

"They certainly are," Ida said. "I never see people kiss like that anymore. They look like they're starring in a forties movie. In an old-fashioned clinch."

"That Roz," Laura said. "She has style."

"How did this coupling come about?" Nina asked.

"According to Roz, it was instant magnetism. They took one look at each other and jumped right into bed. They've hardly gotten out since. She says she has to force herself to even get up to go to the bathroom."

"But how did they meet?" Nina asked.

"She said that Peter flipped out when he heard that she was accusing the animal rights people of murdering Andy. He didn't want his organization implicated, so he took it upon himself to go over and have a chat with her. According to Roz, he left two days later."

"But Andy hasn't been dead that long," Nina said. "Doesn't she feel funny about getting . . . um . . . back in the saddle again so soon?"

"Roz isn't the kind of person you'd expect to stay celibate very long," Laura said.

"As opposed to who? Me?" Nina regretted the words before she even finished speaking them.

"Well, I bet you could go longer than Roz, sweetie pie." Laura pinched Nina's cheek.

"Oh, for godsakes," Ida said. "Stop carrying on. So you're in the normal range. Somewhere between Emily Dickinson and Roz Brillstein. What's wrong with that?"

"I'm not taking any advice from someone who's gone more than a decade without getting laid," Nina said.

"Oh, I used to look around after your father died. I'd sit on the bus, in the movies, and in my *alter kocker* continuing ed classrooms. And all I'd see was a bunch of old men with hair growing out of their ears and noses. Half of them asleep in their seats. And you know, they all smell faintly of *pishochs* from their prostate problems."

"Great attitude," Nina said. "With a mother like you, it's no wonder I'm doomed to a life of celibacy."

"Please, Nina," Laura said, "spare me. How long has it been since you left California. Three months?"

"Less than that."

"And you think that's a world record? Plenty of married people I know can beat it."

"So I guess you don't consider marriage to be a cure for celibacy."

"Not necessarily," Laura said.

"Besides," their mother added, "it's often a temporary solution. Look at me."

"I'll bet that Roz is still bringing home men from bars while she's on Medicare," Nina said.

"Roz is a sexual virtuoso." Laura flung her hands around for emphasis. "A regular YoYo Ma in bed."

"So's Peter Slater," Nina said. "At least that was the impression I got."

"So there you go," Ida said. "Two extremely talented people playing a brilliant duet."

"But I want to play too," Nina sighed.

The three woman watched Roz run her hand through Peter's hair. "Look at us," Ida said finally. "We each look like a kid with his nose pressed up against a candy store window."

"Or cousin Stephanie eyeing a Donna Karan trunk show," Nina said.

"Well, who wouldn't want to have a sex life like Roz's?" Laura whined. "It's like looking at a thousand-dollar cashmere jacket when you're wearing a sweater from the Gap."

"Or have to go around stark naked," Nina said. "Like me."

"I'm not going to try and compete with you, Nina," Laura said. "But I might add that what you've lacked in consistency, you've more than made up for in variety."

"You think I wouldn't have married myself off to a doctor in my twenties if I had had the opportunity?"

"You think my life's been so easy?"

"Here they go," Ida said. "My two girls, squabbling about who has the more wretched existence. My heart bleeds for you both."

Nina and Laura looked down at their shoes, as if they had just been chastised by their fourth-grade teacher.

"You know what you remind me of?" Ida said. "That old joke about the shtetl."

"Which one?" It seemed to Nina that all old jokes were

either about the shtetl or about elderly impotent men who seek cures at the urologist.

"There were two farmers. One had two cows, the other had only one. All his life, the farmer with the one cow was consumed with jealousy for his neighbor. One day, he's digging around in the cowshit and he finds a magic lamp. He rubs it and a genie pops out."

"They had genies in the shtetl?"

"Yeah, but not enough to go around. Anyway, the genie says that he can grant the farmer one wish. The farmer is ecstatic. 'Thank god you came along, genie. All my life I've been jealous of my neighbor. Now my life will be worth living again.' 'So what is it that you want?' the genie asks. 'Isn't it obvious?' the farmer says. 'Kill one of his cows.'"

"We're not that bad, are we?" Laura asked.

But Nina knew that her mother was right. The whining about weight, money, and men was starting to feel like an act. The truth was that Nina was thrilled to be back in Manhattan and profoundly grateful for the opportunity to explore a new career.

But she had been looking at the glass as half empty for so long, she had a feeling that it was too late to change. Training herself to see it as half full would be like learning a new language. And she was just too old to become bilingual. Perhaps she'd be able to pick up a few words, but Nina knew that she'd never be fluent.

"C'mon, Ma," Nina said. "Just because you feel blessed doesn't mean you can't complain."

"Would you like me to cross-stitch a sampler for you?" Ida asked.

Laura laughed. Ida changed the subject. "Actually, a couple of things make sense now," she said.

"Like what?"

"Well, for one thing, now we know why Roz made a

one-hundred-and-eighty-degree turn on her suspicions. She was so adamant about those animal rights people and then she completely withdrew her allegation. I didn't understand it at the time. Now I see why."

"Yeah, Peter really got to her," Laura said.

"So to speak. Also," Ida continued, "I think that Elliott had something to do with those suspicions in the first place. He was probably fueling her paranoia, fabricating incidents and pretending that Andy was the recipient of all sorts of threats."

"You think so?"

"Yeah, he had to in order to create an obvious group of suspects and get the heat off himself. He knew Roz was an easy target, with her inherent hatred of SPASM and AFTA. She is, after all, the daughter of a furrier."

"You're right," Nina said. "Apparently there were a few incidents, but they were minor and happened a while ago. It must have been Elliott who distorted and blew them out of proportion. You know what's funny about the way this whole thing has played out?"

"What?"

"After all my suspicions, my doubts about Peter Slater, Dottie Daley, Roz herself, about Tina and David, even about Bob and Lou Campbell, the one thing that turned out to be true was something that Dottie said early on. And I just dismissed her, assuming she was a nut."

"What did she say?"

"If you want to find the killer, take a look at the people who kill small mammals for a living."

"That's not technically correct," Ida said. "The killer was actually someone who shrunk small mammals for a living."

"You know I take strong issue with that," Laura said. "Nina, you wouldn't be so blasé about medical research if you had kids. Then you'd be more worried about infectious diseases than about the lives of a few mice."

Nina hated it when Laura got on her "I've procreated and you haven't" high horse. But Nina decided to let it pass. It was a New Year. It was almost a new century. A hundred years ago, her grandmother had been sick as a dog in steerage, hoping to be able to work fourteen-hour shifts in a sweatshop so that one day her granddaughters could snip at each other over homemade focaccia. Maybe being blessed didn't mean you could still complain. Maybe it was time to give it up. Funny, this was the first time Nina had ever really considered it.

Match wits with the best-selling

MYSTERY WRITERS

in the business!

SUSAN DUNLAP

"Dunlap's police procedurals have the authenticity of telling detail."
—*The Washington Post Book World*

☐ AS A FAVOR	20999-4	$4.99
☐ ROGUE WAVE	21197-2	$4.99
☐ DEATH AND TAXES	21406-8	$4.99
☐ HIGHFALL	21560-9	$5.50

SARA PARETSKY

"Paretsky's name always makes the top of the list when people talk about the new female operatives." —*The New York Times Book Review*

☐ BLOOD SHOT	20420-8	$6.99
☐ BURN MARKS	20845-9	$6.99
☐ INDEMNITY ONLY	21069-0	$6.99
☐ GUARDIAN ANGEL	21399-1	$6.99
☐ KILLING ORDERS	21528-5	$6.99
☐ DEADLOCK	21332-0	$6.99
☐ TUNNEL VISION	21752-0	$6.99

SISTER CAROL ANNE O'MARIE

"Move over Miss Marple..." —*San Francisco Sunday Examiner & Chronicle*

☐ ADVENT OF DYING	10052-6	$4.99
☐ THE MISSING MADONNA	20473-9	$4.99
☐ A NOVENA FOR MURDER	16469-9	$4.99
☐ MURDER IN ORDINARY TIME	21353-3	$4.99
☐ MURDER MAKES A PILGRIMAGE	21613-3	$4.99

LINDA BARNES

☐ COYOTE	21089-5	$4.99
☐ STEEL GUITAR	21268-5	$4.99
☐ BITTER FINISH	21606-0	$4.99
☐ SNAPSHOT	21220-0	$5.99